He's stalking the twins . . .

. . . and he's closer than ever.

Gradually, Elizabeth slipped back into a troubled sleep, only to be visited again by the nightmare she'd had as the full moon hung over Pembroke Manor, the night Joy Singleton was murdered in Jessica's bed. Elizabeth stood helpless as the werewolf chased her sister, as he grasped Jessica with hairy, muscular arms, as he bent with a howl to tear her throat with his teeth. . . .

Wait a minute. . . . In her dream, Elizabeth heard the snarl close to her own ear; she felt the claws digging into her flesh, the hot breath against her throat, the point of a knife-sharp fang. This time, the girl the werewolf was pursuing was herself.

BEWARE THE WOLFMAN

Written by
Kate William

Created by
FRANCINE PASCAL

BANTAM BOOKS
NEW YORK · TORONTO · LONDON · SYDNEY · AUCKLAND

RL 6, age 12 and up

BEWARE THE WOLFMAN
A Bantam Book / June 1994

Sweet Valley High® *is a registered trademark of Francine Pascal*
Conceived by Francine Pascal
Produced by Daniel Weiss Associates, Inc.
33 West 17th Street
New York, NY 10011
Cover art by Bruce Emmett

ISBN: 0-553-56234-7

Published simultaneously in the United States and Canada

Bantam Books are published by Bantam Books, a division of Bantam
Doubleday Dell Publishing Group, Inc. Its trademark, consisting of the
words "Bantam Books" and the portrayal of a rooster, is Registered in
U.S. Patent and Trademark Office and in other countries. Marca
Registrada. Bantam Books, 1540 Broadway, New York, New York 10036.

PRINTED IN THE UNITED STATES OF AMERICA

OPM   0 9 8 7 6 5 4 3 2 1

To John Stewart Carmen

Chapter 1

Sixteen-year-old Elizabeth Wakefield passed a platter of warm breakfast scones to her Housing for International Students roommate, aspiring young actress Portia Albert. After choosing a plump raisin scone, Portia passed the platter along to freckled, auburn-haired Emily Cartwright.

"I wonder what Lina's having for breakfast this morning?" mused Emily as she added a scone to her plate, already piled high with farm-style bacon, eggs over easy, and juicy broiled tomatoes.

Elizabeth's blue-green eyes crinkled in a smile. "You mean Eliana. Princess Eliana."

"She's probably having the same thing we are," Portia guessed. "Only, she's eating her eggs with a silver fork from a solid-gold dish."

The three girls laughed merrily. "I don't think snooty old Mrs. Bates will ever recover from learn-

1

ing that the Queen of England's daughter was living in her dormitory," said Elizabeth, pushing back a long strand of golden blond hair. "And the whole time, she'd been looking down her nose at her, thinking Lina was just a poor working-class girl from Liverpool!"

"She practically fainted when she saw the special edition of the *London Journal* with your article," Emily agreed. "Her fat old face turned white and then purple and then green. If there hadn't been a chair right behind her, she would have fallen flat on the floor."

"Maybe Mrs. Bates will learn a lesson," Portia speculated, filling her cup with steaming hot tea. "In the future, I wager she won't be so quick to play favorites based on whether she thinks one of her boarders is well born or well connected!"

Emily nodded, her green eyes twinkling mischievously. "Now, if I can only convince her I'm the runaway daughter of the Queen of Australia . . . !"

Elizabeth shook her head, smiling. The story really was like a fairy tale. When Elizabeth and her twin sister, Jessica, arrived at HIS a few weeks earlier, their home for the time they'd spend as interns at a London newspaper, the housemother, Mrs. Bates, had assigned them to a room with Portia Albert and Lina Smith. Elizabeth had struck up a friendship with Lina immediately, admiring the sweet, plainspoken girl with mousy brown hair and wire-rimmed glasses who was devoting her

2

summer to helping at a homeless shelter and soup kitchen.

From the start, though, there had been something a bit puzzling, a bit off, about Lina. "Remember when you found that fancy cocktail dress in the back of the closet?" Elizabeth asked Emily. "And Lina had such elegant nightgowns—not at all what you'd think a girl from a poor family would wear."

"And you noticed that her glasses had clear lenses," said Emily.

Portia tossed her glossy raven hair. "And we all noticed that she had a mad crush on David Bartholomew but for some mysterious reason wouldn't do anything about it."

Emily grinned. "Plus, it always seemed funny to me that Lina should know more high-society gossip than me, seeing as how I've been known to spend every spare moment reading about the royals in the tabloids!"

"When she told me who she really was, that night before we went to the opening of your play," Elizabeth said to Portia, "I almost pulled a Mrs. Bates and fainted dead away. It was the hardest secret I ever had to keep."

"Especially with huge headlines in the paper every day," said Portia. "Her disappearance was the biggest news to hit London in ages."

"All's well that ends well," Elizabeth concluded. "She's back with her family at Buckingham Palace,

3

but she's determined to stay in touch with the real world and the causes she cares about. She and David fell in love and they don't care in the least that their backgrounds are so different. And finally, when David received the one-million-pound reward for finding the princess, he turned right around and donated it to the homeless shelter!"

Portia stirred a spoonful of sugar into her tea. "It's absolutely the most romantic story, like something from a play."

"Maybe it will be a play," said Emily. "It could be your next stage role, Porsh!"

Lina's not the only one who surprised us, thought Elizabeth, digging into her bacon and eggs. Portia wasn't the girl they'd all thought her to be, either. The daughter of the incomparable Shakespearean actor Sir Montford Albert, who directed a theater company in Edinburgh, Scotland, Portia had come to London to launch her own acting career. Right away, she'd landed a role in a new West End play . . . on the basis of her famous name rather than on her talent, her fellow HIS residents had assumed. There wasn't much incentive to give Portia the benefit of the doubt; she was arrogant and pretentious and cold as ice, disdaining to socialize the least little bit with the other teenagers at HIS.

Then, the day of her opening night, she left complimentary tickets for us, Elizabeth remembered. Elizabeth had managed to talk Jessica, Emily, David, and Gabriello into giving Portia one last chance. At the theater, they'd been astounded to discover that Portia was performing under an alias: Penelope Abbott. Not only that, but the personality of Isabelle in *A Common Man* was uncannily like Portia's own personality . . . or what they'd all assumed was her personality.

"You fooled us, too, Portia," Elizabeth said out loud. "We thought Isabelle Huntington was the real you!"

Portia smiled ruefully. "I wanted so much to prove myself to the world . . . and to my father. The only way I knew to really excel in my art was to immerse myself one hundred percent in the role. I'm only glad you were willing to forgive me for practicing my lines on you!"

"I almost didn't," Emily teased. "You were a real pain in the derriere, Portia Albert!"

Portia flashed an endearing smile and patted Emily's arm. "But we're friends now, aren't we? That's why I told my father I don't want to move into the fancy flat he found for me on the other side of town."

"What fancy flat?" asked Elizabeth.

"After seeing the play the other night and realizing not only am I serious about becoming an actress, but I may actually be good at it, he's suddenly behind me heart and soul and pocketbook. You saw the flowers upstairs?"

"How could I miss them?" Elizabeth laughed. "That bouquet is bigger than I am!"

"It came with a card from my parents," Portia explained, "offering to rent me a place of my own, so I could have more privacy than here at the dorm."

Elizabeth's face fell. The third-floor bedroom already seemed empty with Lina gone. "You're not leaving, too, are you?"

Portia shook her head firmly. "I told them I'm happy where I am—I'm happy sharing digs with all of you. Your friendship helps keep me going, gets me up on that stage every night. No, I'm not budging." She grinned. "You're stuck with me!"

"I'm glad," Elizabeth said. "Because—"

Just then, the dining-room door swung open. David Bartholomew and Gabriello Moretti sprinted in, each waving a couple of newspapers. "Wait until you see these headlines," David called. "They're even bigger than the ones about the missing Princess!"

Elizabeth's heart sank. She already knew what the headlines would say. *If only I could wake up one morning and find it's all been a dream,* she thought, forcing herself to look at the newspapers the boys tossed on the table. *A terrible, terrible dream.*

The *London Journal* was uppermost, its lead story titled, "Young Lord Pembroke Suspect in Murder Case." The sensational *London Daily Post* used all capital letters for added drama: "WERE-WOLF STALKS LONDON BY NIGHT!" A three-inch-high headline in yet another newspaper asked, "Little Lord Pembroke: Werewolf?"

Elizabeth pushed the newspapers away, and her plate as well. Her appetite had vanished. "It's almost worse than not knowing who the killer was, to have it turn out to be him."

Emily clucked her tongue sadly. "Your poor, poor sister."

"Well, the man's innocent until proven guilty, isn't he?" said David, pulling up a chair.

"Yes," Portia agreed. "But is there really any doubt?"

Her expression grim, Elizabeth shook her head. "I wish there was still room for doubt—I'd give anything to believe the murderer wasn't Robert Pembroke." *The boy my sister's fallen in love with . . .* "But the evidence all points in his direction. His own father admits as much."

As her eye was drawn back to the newspaper headlines, Elizabeth's thoughts returned to the beginning of it all. Their very first day at the *Journal*, she and Jessica had taken it upon themselves to sneak over to the scene of a major crime. A prominent London physician had been brutally murdered and, spying through a window, the twins had seen his corpse. His throat had been ripped open, as if by a wild beast.

After that, events began to snowball. *Journal* editor-in-chief Henry Reeves drastically cut and altered crime editor Lucy Friday's article about Dr.

7

Neville's murder. Lucy in turn accused Reeves of conspiring in a cover-up with the *Journal's* owner, Lord Robert Pembroke, and the London chief of police, and then quit her position. More bodies began to turn up, all killed in the same savage manner. And one of the victims was murdered in the very bed Jessica was supposed to be sleeping in at Pembroke Manor. . . .

Elizabeth shuddered, remembering the previous weekend. Jessica had been invited to the Pembrokes' country estate by Lord Pembroke's son and heir, Robert, and she'd talked Elizabeth and Elizabeth's friend from work, Luke Shepherd, into going with her. For Elizabeth and Luke, it was a chance to investigate the Pembroke family—to find out if there was any truth to Lucy Friday's theory that the Pembrokes had something to hide.

It was the night of the full moon, Elizabeth recalled. And the local constable came by the manor to tell Lord Pembroke that some sheep had been found on his property, slaughtered. Luke was sure it was a werewolf, and then she'd had that horrible dream. . . .

She'd dreamed that Jessica was being pursued by a werewolf, and she herself could only watch helplessly. When she woke the next morning and ran to her sister's room, it looked for a minute as if the dream had become reality. A girl with blond hair lay on the bed in a pool of blood . . . dead.

It turned out that Jessica had switched rooms

with another guest—the victim was actually Joy Singleton, fiancée of London police chief Andrew Thatcher. Soon the local police were on the case, but Elizabeth had decided to do some sleuthing on her own. Returning to Pembroke Manor, she'd discovered a hidden room filled with books about werewolves—Lord Pembroke had a passionate, perhaps obsessive, interest in the subject.

She'd also overheard a bone-chilling conversation between Lord Pembroke Senior and Thatcher. It turned out Pembroke had been hiding something—he'd been using his personal influence over Thatcher to stall the police investigation of the killings so he could gather clues and capture the werewolf himself. But with another dead body at Pembroke Manor, that of the Pembroke Manor cook, Thatcher finally persuaded Lord Pembroke to turn his evidence over to the police . . . and announce at a press conference that his own son, Robert Junior, was the number one suspect.

"We'd better put these away in case Jessica—" Emily began.

She didn't get a chance to finish her sentence. At that moment, Jessica herself entered the dining room.

Before Emily and the others could shove the newspapers under the table, Jessica charged over and snatched one of them up. Two spots of angry pink blossomed in her cheeks as she scanned the headline.

9

"Are you happy, Liz?" Jessica demanded, flinging the paper at her sister. "Are you pleased with what you've done?"

An awkward silence fell over the dining room. "I haven't done anything," Elizabeth said quietly.

"Oh, no?" Jessica put her hands on her hips, her eyes shooting sparks. "You and all your snooping around at Pembroke Manor. You wouldn't rest until you'd pinned this on Robert and his family. And then you and Luke forced your absurd, demented werewolf theory on everybody!"

"We didn't force any theory on anyone," Elizabeth protested. "The press jumped to their own conclusions, given the evidence."

"Well, they're wrong. You're all wrong! Robert Pembroke isn't a killer, much less a werewolf. You've ruined an innocent man's life, Elizabeth," Jessica cried passionately, "and you've ruined my life, too!"

At this, Elizabeth lost what grasp she had left on her temper. She jumped to her feet to stand face-to-face with her sister. "I've ruined your life? I'm trying to save your life, you idiot!" she shouted. "I can't believe how deluded you are!"

"I'm deluded, says the girl who believes in werewolves. I'm deluded!"

"Yes, you are," Elizabeth snapped. "All the evidence points to Robert. He had the opportunity to commit the murders. His cigarette case was found near Dr. Neville's body—threads from his bathrobe turned up on the door frame of your room at Pembroke Manor. And now he's skipped town, disappeared without a trace. If that doesn't prove he's guilty, nothing does, and if you weren't so blinded by his money and title, you'd see what everybody else sees."

"He didn't do it," Jessica insisted stubbornly.

Elizabeth's hands clenched into fists. She resisted the urge to grab her sister and shake her hard. "How can you defend him, Jess, when he tried to kill you, too, first at Pembroke Manor and then again the other day in the tube station?"

"It wasn't Robert who attacked me!" Jessica cried. "How many times do I have to say that? You're not even listening to me. The case is closed in your opinion. Robert is your idea of the perfect villain, isn't he? You disliked him on principle from the beginning."

"I did not," protested Elizabeth.

"You did, too. You're the worst kind of reverse snob, Liz. Because he's rich, you just assumed Robert was selfish and shallow and utterly without morals. Well, I'll tell you something that may shock you," Jessica said, in her most bitterly sarcastic tone. "Having money doesn't make a person bad, any more than people without money are automatically saints."

Elizabeth's eyes flashed indignantly at this disparaging allusion to Luke. "Don't even think about trying to drag Luke down to Robert's level. He's as

11

good as they come, but then, you wouldn't know that. You've never given him the time of day because his name isn't *Lord* Shepherd."

"Luke may be as good as they come, but he's also a nut, if you ask me," countered Jessica. "You're both nuts. And you're lousy reporters. You think you're hot stuff, though, don't you, Liz? Getting your byline on that front-page article about Princess Eliana. Boy, it must have been tough to crack that case, seeing as how Lina came right out and told you who she really was! You'll have to work a lot harder to prove Robert's guilty, because the evidence you keep harping on is totally inconclusive and you couldn't come up with a motive if your life depended on it."

With that, Jessica dropped into a chair, folding her arms across her chest. Elizabeth stared down at her sister. Her mouth opened and closed—she was still seething—but she'd run out of arguments. As usual, she'd gotten nowhere fast trying to reason with Jessica.

What's the point of wasting my breath? Elizabeth wondered, grabbing her shoulder bag. *She doesn't want my help—she doesn't deserve my help.*

"See ya, Emily, Portia, David, Gabriello," said Elizabeth. Pointedly ignoring her sister, Elizabeth spun on her heel and stomped off. *I'm not waiting for her,* she decided. *I'm not riding to work with her. In fact, I'm not speaking to her ever again!*

Jessica glared after her sister, her eyes narrowed into angry slits. *This is it,* she fumed silently. *This is really it, once and for all. I'm not speaking to that girl again for as long as I live!*

It wasn't the first time the twins had knocked heads about something. Their faces and figures might be identical, but their minds definitely were not. Over the course of sixteen action-packed years, they'd fought over toys, clothes, boys, friends, the phone, the car. *We usually fight because Miss Goody Two-Shoes is too stuffy and serious and responsible to see anybody else's point of view,* Jessica thought. Everything blew over eventually . . . when Elizabeth would finally lighten up and see reason. But Jessica had a feeling this fight wasn't going to blow over. It was the worst one ever.

David and Gabriello, both summer students at London University, hoisted their backpacks and waved good-bye. Jessica watched the boys go, her anger slowly draining away. With a heavy sigh, she slumped forward, her elbows on the table and her head in her hands.

She'd just woken up, but she felt as if she'd already run a marathon—because she knew what an uphill battle she faced. *How can I prove Robert's innocent after everything that's happened?* Jessica wondered bleakly. *Everyone assumes his father tipped him off and he skipped town to save his skin. Where is he?* Tears smarted in her eyes as she remembered Robert's sudden departure, his air of

13

mystery as he said good-bye to her two days ago. *Why didn't he tell me what was going on? Why did he leave me, alone and in the dark?*

On the other side of the table, Emily cleared her throat. "You probably won't want to hear this, Jessica," she began.

Jessica lifted her head. "Then don't say it," she advised coolly. "If you want to make accusations against Robert, go talk to Elizabeth."

"It's not that at all," Emily insisted, putting a hand on her friend's arm. "I just think you should be careful. I'm worried about you."

"Liz is right about that, at least," Portia agreed. "Someone did try to kill you. If you hadn't switched rooms with Joy Singleton . . ."

"It wasn't Robert," Jessica repeated. She sounded like a broken record, but she didn't care. She'd keep saying it until someone believed her. "It wasn't Robert. I know him. He loves me."

Her friends nodded sympathetically, but Jessica could tell they weren't convinced. Their doubts were written all over their faces. *They're thinking maybe I know him, but not well enough. They're thinking evidence is evidence.*

It was true, she and Robert had only been dating for a few weeks. All Jessica really had to go on was a gut instinct, but it was a strong one. *He's a good person, no matter what Liz says. Sure, he was wild as a kid, getting kicked out of school and stuff like that, but that hardly makes him homicidal ma-*

14

niac material. If he'd wanted to harm her, he'd had plenty of chances. Far from threatening her, though, the last time she saw him, Robert had been concerned about nothing but her safety.

No, Jessica was willing to stake her life that Robert Pembroke was not the werewolf of London. Which meant somebody else was. . . .

"I'm glad it's the weekend," Luke Shepherd said to Elizabeth as they strolled through the park down the street from HIS late Friday afternoon. "I'm ready for a few days off, aren't you?"

Turning up the collar of her jacket, Elizabeth nodded. "Things have been crazier than ever at the *Journal* since Reeves got the boot."

"What a turnaround on Lord Pembroke's part," Luke remarked. "One minute, he's masterminding a cover-up of the murders, the next he's publicly backing the police search for his son and firing Reeves for obeying his orders."

"It was one thing to play down the Neville murder, but Reeves went too far when he took it upon himself to print an unsubstantiated story about the princess," Elizabeth reminded Luke. "Lord Pembroke didn't order him to do that. Reeves just got carried away trying to compete with the *London Daily Post.* Too bad, too. He sabotaged a long, distinguished career."

"Well, one thing's for certain," said Luke, wrapping an arm around Elizabeth's shoulders. "There

15

hasn't been a dull moment since you started your internship!"

"There hasn't," she agreed wholeheartedly. Because not only had she gotten caught up on the hunt for a savage serial killer, but she'd fallen head over heels for an adorable English boy.

Elizabeth looked up at Luke and he smiled down at her. In the misty gray dusk, with his fair skin, dark hair, lake-blue eyes, and rosy lips, he looked more than ever like the romantic hero of a nineteenth-century novel. Elizabeth's heart did a somersault. She hadn't come to London looking for a boyfriend—she had one at home, and she'd intended to be faithful to him. But she couldn't help the way Luke made her feel. They had so much in common—a love of literature and history—so much to talk about. And when he put his arms around her, the rest of the world—including Todd Wilkins back in Sweet Valley, California—disappeared.

It was a typical gray, drizzly London evening, but Luke's embrace warmed Elizabeth like a fire. They kissed and then continued strolling, hand in hand.

"I didn't see Jessica around the office much today," Luke remarked. "How is she handling all this?"

"She's not," Elizabeth said, frowning. "We had a total blowup this morning about it. She just won't let go of Robert."

"Are you two on the outs?"

"That's a nice way of putting it. I'm so frustrated with her! But I'm worried, too," Elizabeth confessed. "She's madly in love with him—she's obsessed. I know she's going to look for him. And I'm afraid she might actually find him."

"Or he might find her," said Luke.

"Right. So that's why I think we should try to track Robert down ourselves," Elizabeth proposed. "If we could help bring him safely into custody—"

Luke halted, gripping Elizabeth's arms with both hands. A gust of wind stirred the wet leaves overhead, showering them both with raindrops. "I don't want you taking any more risks," he told her with uncharacteristic sternness. "The police department and Scotland Yard are in charge of the case now. Promise me you won't strike off on your own and put yourself in danger."

Luke folded her in a protective hug. Elizabeth rested her head against his chest. "I promise," she said, feeling guilty about the fib. Because despite Luke's misgivings, she was determined. She couldn't just stand by and do nothing. *I've got to find Robert,* she thought, staring past Luke's shoulder at a homeless man in a shabby brown coat and cap, poking around in the leaves with a stick. *Jessica won't be safe until he's behind bars.*

Stepping back slightly, Luke placed a hand under Elizabeth's chin and lifted her face to his. "I'm serious about this, Liz," he said. "With Robert named as the chief suspect and on the run, both you and Jessica need to be more careful than ever. Robert knows you helped turn up the evidence against him—he could seek revenge."

Elizabeth thought about Maria Finch, formerly the cook at Pembroke Manor, and shivered. Maria had seen something the night of Joy Singleton's murder, but before she could cast any light on the case, she, too, had been murdered. Silenced. Her throat torn open.

"I'm . . . I'm afraid," Elizabeth whispered.

Luke ran a finger gently down the side of her face to her throat. "I know you are." He touched the pendant she wore around her neck. "Remember when I gave this to you?"

Elizabeth nodded. The antique silver pendant was etched with the image of a wolf enclosed in a pentagram. Luke had given it to her as they strolled through the woods near Pembroke Manor. He thought there might be danger because they had seen wolfsbane in bloom and there was going to be a full moon. And he was right.

"I told you it would protect you," said Luke, "neutralize the werewolf's power, and it will if you continue to wear it night and day. But the danger is growing fiercer all the time."

He reached into his pocket and then pressed something cold and metallic into Elizabeth's palm. She opened her fingers, exclaiming, "A silver bullet!"

"One of the few weapons that can destroy a werewolf," Luke confirmed.

Elizabeth and Luke had held many conversations about werewolves. His mother, who died when he was young, had imbued him with a passionate interest in folklore; because of his poetic nature, he seemed to respond to the legends as reality rather than myth. From the beginning, Luke had been convinced that the string of barbaric murders was the work of a werewolf.

Jessica's sarcastic comments darted through Elizabeth's brain. *Absurd, demented, deluded . . .* She knew she should be skeptical, but not for the first time, she felt herself falling under the spell of Luke's convictions. An icy chill swept through her body even as she forced a laugh. "What good is a silver bullet without a gun?"

"Carry it in your pocket," Luke insisted. "He'll know that you have it, that you have the power to destroy him. Keep it with you. Just trust me."

Elizabeth looked up into Luke's anxious, sincere eyes and nodded. She did trust him, implicitly.

In all the strange, swirling mist of violence—of terror, mystery, and suspicion—she was certain of only one thing: her feelings for Luke Shepherd and his feelings for her. *He's been with me every step of the way,* she thought, slipping the silver bullet into her pocket and then throwing her arms around Luke. *He'll see me through this. He'll protect me.*

Chapter 2

Waking up Saturday morning, Elizabeth was glad to look out the window by her bed and see the rain had cleared.

"What a wonderful day to visit Buckingham Palace," said Portia, who was sitting at her dressing table brushing her long, dark hair. "I can't tell you how envious I am!"

Elizabeth hopped out of bed, stretching her arms over her head. "I wish you could come with us."

"If I didn't have a matinee performance, it would be jolly," Portia agreed. She winked. "Be sure to give my regards to the queen."

Out of the corner of her eye, Elizabeth saw Jessica roll over in the top bunk and pull a pillow over her head. Portia pointed to Jessica, mouthing the words, "Is she going?"

Elizabeth shrugged. "I have no idea," she whispered. "We're not speaking to each other."

Portia clucked her tongue. "Not speaking? Why, Liz, you oughtn't let one little row—"

"It wasn't a little row," Elizabeth interrupted, loud enough for her sister to hear. "It's probably best if you don't get involved, Portia," she advised. "That way, you won't have to choose sides."

Portia put down her hairbrush and gazed at Elizabeth, her gray eyes cloudy with concern. "I just don't like to see—"

Elizabeth cut Portia off again. "I'm going to take a shower," she said, grabbing her bathrobe and breezing toward the door. "Have a nice day."

An hour later, as she and David sped to the royal residence in the car Eliana had sent for them, Elizabeth thought back to the scene earlier that morning. *I was kind of rude to Portia,* she thought ruefully. *It's not her fault she's caught in the middle—she just wants to make peace.*

Elizabeth pictured her sister, burrowing under the bedclothes like a crab in the sand, and she felt another pang. *Should I have called a truce? If Jess were going to the palace with me, at least I'd know she was staying out of trouble. . . .*

David had been looking out the car window in silence. Now he turned to Elizabeth. "My palms are sweating," he confessed. "I don't know if I have the nerve to date a princess."

"It's pretty daunting," Elizabeth commiserated.

22

"Meeting your girlfriend's mother . . . the Queen of England!"

"What if . . . what if her, Eliana's, feelings have changed?" David ran a hand through his straw-colored hair and then tugged nervously at the collar of his shirt. "I haven't seen her since she moved back home a couple of days ago. What if it doesn't make sense to her anymore, hanging out with an ordinary bloke like me?"

Elizabeth patted David's knee. "She'll feel exactly the same way she did when she was Lina Smith, working at the soup kitchen and sleeping in the bunk above Portia," Elizabeth promised. "She doesn't care about artificial social distinctions. That's why she ran away from home in the first place—to escape, to experience the real world, to establish an identity for herself apart from the royal family."

David smiled. "She's really something, isn't she?"

"She's one in a million. And she's wild about you."

"I'm still nervous about meeting the queen."

"No kidding." Elizabeth laughed. "I'm terrified!"

David grew even more jittery five minutes later, when a palace guard waved them through the gate. "We're having tea with the queen," he muttered, pink spots of excitement rising in his fair cheeks. "Every single citizen of England dreams of doing that, and it's happening to me, David Bartholomew!"

Elizabeth clasped her hands in her lap, her own

eyes bright with anticipation. What a story to tell her friends back home! Tea with the queen would definitely be the highlight of their day with Eliana. At the same time . . .

Elizabeth resisted an impulse to ask the driver to turn around and take her back to HIS. *Tea with the queen—is that really important?* she thought guiltily. *How can I goof off like this when people are dying . . . when my own sister might be next?* Sure, it would be fun and unforgettable to visit Princess Eliana at Buckingham Palace. Elizabeth bit her lip. *But I should be looking for Robert. I should be out there trying to solve this mystery.*

"Do you want to help me with my lines or not?" Portia asked somewhat peevishly.

It was late Saturday afternoon, and the two girls were sitting in Portia's dressing room backstage at the Ravensgate Theatre. For lack of anything else to do, Jessica had dropped by to gab with Portia in between the matinee and evening performances of *A Common Man.*

Now Jessica heaved a sigh, frowning at her copy of the script of Portia's play. "Sorry. I'm just a little distracted."

Portia arched one slender, sardonic eyebrow. "Really? I hadn't noticed."

"Let's try it again," Jessica offered. "From the beginning of the scene, when you come in from the garden."

24

Portia closed her script. "Actually, I think I'd like to leave it for now. I may change an inflection—a gesture—a little something, just to keep it from feeling stale. But not tonight."

Tossing down the script, Jessica glanced at the clock on the wall. It was four thirty—teatime. At that very moment, Elizabeth was probably perched on a velvet chair, sipping from a delicate china cup, her pinkie finger lifted, making conversation with the Queen of England.

It should have been me, Jessica thought petulantly. *What does Liz know or care about the royal family?* But she'd vowed not to be in the same room as her sister . . . and that included throne rooms.

"You're not doing anyone any good by moping, you know," Portia said as she leaned close to the mirror to touch up her mascara. "Do something productive."

Crossing her arms, Jessica pushed out her lower lip in a classic pout. "Like what?"

"Use your noodle," Portia suggested bluntly. "Do you want to help clear Robert's name so he can come out of hiding or not?"

Jessica sighed. Clear Robert's name . . . come out of hiding . . . It all sounded so dire and melodramatic. How on earth had they gotten into this predicament?

The *London Journal* internship had started out so fabulously. Her very first day on the job, she was sent to write up a story at Pembroke Green, the el-

25

egant London residence of the landed-gentry Pembroke family, distant relatives of the Windsors. She'd met Lord and Lady Pembroke's aristocratic only son, Robert, and he'd taken her to tea . . . and then dinner . . . and then dancing. He'd swept her off her feet, just like in a fairy tale. Jessica had found her Prince Charming.

Visiting the Pembrokes' country estate was supposed to be the most romantic and incredible experience of my life, she reflected morosely. Instead, Luke and Elizabeth and some insane murderer had turned it into a werewolf festival. Now the whole city of London was up in arms . . . and the love of her life was public enemy number one.

Portia tipped her head to one side, thoughtful eyes resting on Jessica's face. "Or maybe you're ready to write off Robert Pembroke," Portia speculated. "Maybe your feelings for him don't run deep enough to warrant unshaking loyalty in the face of the crimes he's being charged with."

"No," Jessica said forcefully. "I'm not writing him off. Sure, I could. Easily. And I would if Elizabeth were right and all I ever cared about was Robert's money and title. But we're in love. My feelings are real. And Robert's innocent."

Portia clapped. "Bravo!"

Jessica smiled ruefully. "What a speech, huh?"

"Now all you have to do is translate that passion into action."

Jessica thought about Elizabeth, taking the investigation into her own hands, snooping around Pembroke Manor scribbling notes and interviewing people. "Liz isn't the only one who can play Nancy Drew," Jessica declared. "If Robert isn't the killer, then someone else is—and it's time Jessica Wakefield, private eye, got to the bottom of things. So, how do I start?"

"How about at the beginning?"

"And in the beginning, there was a body." Jessica nodded thoughtfully. "And another body, and another . . ."

Her shoulder bag was slung over the back of a director's chair, and now Jessica reached into it to grab the small spiral notebook she used at work. Whipping it open to a blank page, she quickly jotted down a list of names. "Nurse Handley, who was attacked at the hospital where she works," she said out loud. "Dr. Neville, killed in his home, which was also his office. And Dr. Neville, by the way, was a close family friend of the Pembrokes. Poo-Poo, Lady Wimpole's Yorkshire terrier. Police chief Thatcher's girlfriend, Joy Singleton—me, almost. Maria Finch, the Pembroke Manor cook."

Portia shuddered. "Somebody's leaving a very bloody trail."

"If it's a trail, it's a pretty crooked one." Jessica tapped her pencil, the wheels in her brain churning. "There must be a thread connecting these victims—a thread that leads back to the killer. But what is it?"

*   *   *

"How was the concert?" Portia asked Gabriello on Sunday morning as the HIS residents yawned over brunch.

"That's right," said Elizabeth. "The music students at the university summer program put on a performance last night. I almost forgot."

"It went well," Gabriello replied. "But you should really ask Jessica and Emily. They came to cheer me on."

"He played first violin and he was fabulous," Emily raved.

"I didn't think classical music could be so exciting," Jessica admitted. "It was almost as cool as a rock concert."

"What about you?" Emily turned to Elizabeth and David. "I was so mad that the BBC made me work yesterday. How was the princess? How was the palace?"

As David launched into a glowing report of their visit with Eliana, Elizabeth peeped at her sister out of the corner of her eye. Munching a bowl of muesli, Jessica feigned disinterest, but Elizabeth could tell she was dying for details.

"You wouldn't believe the furniture," David gushed, "and the art. Old Master paintings and sculpture and tapestries all over the place. And Eliana's apartment . . . her closet alone is the size of this dining room. She must have a thousand formal gowns."

"Really?" Spoon in hand, Jessica stared at David with round, curious eyes. "What did they look like?"

"I'm the wrong one to ask," said David. "Fashion isn't exactly my bag. Maybe Elizabeth could describe some of them."

Elizabeth glanced coolly at Jessica. Jessica narrowed her eyes. "I guess I'm not that interested after all," Jessica said with a sniff.

Emily hurried to change the subject. "Speaking of fashion, anyone up for a shopping expedition this afternoon?"

"I am," said Jessica.

"Grand. I know you've got a performance, Portia. How 'bout you, Liz?"

Shopping had never been Elizabeth's favorite activity. *And I'm certainly not going if she is,* Elizabeth thought. *Nice try, Em.* Besides, even though Sunday was supposed to be a day of rest and recreation, Elizabeth had serious plans. She had to make up for lost time. "Luke and I are going to the British Museum," she fibbed. "Thanks, anyway."

As Emily and Jessica discussed which stores to target, Elizabeth mentally mapped out her own agenda. *A shopping expedition—perfect!* she thought. *That should keep her out of the way while I do some sleuthing.*

As soon as she and Emily rounded the block

and were out of sight of HIS, Jessica stopped dead in her tracks. She looked both ways to make sure the coast was clear. She didn't want Elizabeth to witness this change in direction and catch on to her scheme.

"What is it?" said Emily, peering nervously into the dense green of the park. "Do you see . . . something?"

"The werewolf?" Jessica laughed. "No, but this is as far as I'm going. I only said yes to the shopping idea to get Elizabeth off my trail. I've got some detective work to do."

"Oh." Emily's face crumpled with disappointment. Then anxiety took its place. "Are you sure it's safe to go off alone?"

"I'll be fine," Jessica assured her. "Just don't tell anyone where I'm going, OK?"

"Where *are* you going?" Emily called as Jessica hurried off.

"See ya!" Jessica yelled back, ignoring her friend's question.

At the corner, Jessica hopped onto a red double-decker bus heading across town. Ten minutes later, she disembarked at Essex Street. She hadn't ventured near the scene of Dr. Neville's murder since the morning she and Elizabeth spied the address in Lucy Friday's datebook and took it upon themselves to investigate. An icy shiver ran up Jessica's spine now as she recalled walking down the tree-lined street . . . sneaking into the cordoned-off yard . . . hiding in the rhododendron

30

bushes . . . looking through the picture window. . . .

"Brr." Jessica forced herself to walk at a brisk, no-nonsense pace, but her teeth were chattering. "Good thing there's no reason to be scared anymore. The bloody corpse won't still be lying on the parlor floor!"

It was a typical cool gray London afternoon, with the ever-present threat of rain. Essex Street appeared deserted. As Jessica approached Dr. Neville's property, she slowed her steps. The gate wasn't blocked by a stern London bobby as on the last occasion, but it was fastened with a giant padlock. Beyond the gate, Jessica could see that the windows of the flat were tightly shuttered. *How on earth am I going to get in there?* she wondered. *And why do I want to get in there?*

She answered her own question. *Because if Robert isn't the werewolf, someone else is, and the best way to clear Robert's name is to unearth the real killer. So, who are my top suspects?*

In her mind, she ran over the list of people who'd been present at Pembroke Manor when Joy Singleton was murdered. *Robert, Lord and Lady Pembroke, Andrew Thatcher, me, Liz, Luke, the servants.* She scratched Elizabeth, Robert, and herself off the list. That left Robert's parents, Joy's fiancé the police chief, Luke, and the Pembroke Manor servants. *Or an outsider,* Jessica conceded with a sigh. *Face it, it could have been just about anyone. Which brings us back to the victims. If I*

31

can just find that thread that connects them . . .
and it's not the thread from Robert's paisley silk
bathrobe, no matter what Liz thinks!

Doubling back along the sidewalk, Jessica
slipped into a narrow alleyway, following it to its
end. On the right, an old brick wall stood between
her and what should be Dr. Neville's backyard.
Good thing I wore sneakers and jeans, Jessica
thought as she climbed the wall, feeling for finger-
and toeholds in the crumbling brick.

Swinging her legs over the top, she dropped
down into the damp, overgrown grass. What a lucky
break! The back windows of the townhouse weren't
shuttered. It took only a minute to jimmy one open
with the knife she'd slipped into her purse that
morning at brunch. Pushing the window up, Jessica
scrambled onto the sill and jumped inside.

She was in the dead man's kitchen. As she
glanced around the dim room, another shiver tick-
led her spine, lifting the hair on the back of her
neck. The table in the breakfast nook was set with
china and silver; a kettle stood on the stove, as if
about to whistle. *Dr. Neville didn't make it to breakfast that morning,* Jessica thought grimly. *Ugh.*

Wandering down the hallway, she peered into
each room. She passed a formal dining room, a film
of dust on the dark mahogany table; the patients'
waiting room, old magazines still fanned out on the
coffee table; an examining room, with instruments
and supplies displayed in a glass-fronted case; the

32

front parlor where the body had been found.

Goose bumps prickled Jessica's arms. She stared at the bare wood floor where at one point a carpet had been . . . a carpet that ended up permanently stained with blood. Outside, the wind stirred the shrubs, causing a branch to tap against the window . . . the very same window she and Elizabeth had gazed through. Jessica jumped. It sounded like a ghostly finger, scratching. . . .

Hurrying away from the parlor, she came to the doctor's study. At the sight of the ornate desk and three tall walnut filing cabinets, her heartbeat quickened. She didn't know exactly what kind of clue she was looking for, but maybe she'd find it here.

The cabinets had four drawers, all stuffed with papers. "Research and journal articles," Jessica muttered, running a finger along the file tabs in the top drawer of the first cabinet. She pulled out the next drawer, and the next. "Accounting and tax stuff—blech."

The second cabinet was more promising. "Patient files!" Jessica's eyes lit up. "This could be it."

She rifled through the folders, searching for anything that might constitute a clue. Not surprisingly, there were files for all the Pembrokes—Neville had been the family physician. "No Handley, though," Jessica observed out loud. "And no Wimpole." She swallowed a nervous giggle. Not that she'd expected to find a file for Poo-Poo—Neville wasn't a vet, after all!

She examined the name on each folder, making her way through the alphabet. Salisbury, Bernard. Sarton, Kendall. Sarton, Meredith. Scofield, Edna. Shafly, Sir Thomas. S., Annabelle.

Jessica paused, frowning at the folder. "S., Annabelle?" she said. "How come Annabelle only gets an initial?" All the other files were headed by the patient's full name.

Curious, Jessica pulled out Annabelle S.'s folder. When she opened it, a single sheet of paper fluttered out onto the floor. Bending, Jessica picked it up. It was a medical chart, mostly blank. The word "deceased" was stamped in red on the top and someone—Dr. Neville, Jessica assumed— had scrawled a brief notation: "cause of death: pneumonia."

Weird, Jessica thought. *How come there are no other charts or forms? Shouldn't there be more stuff about a patient Dr. Neville had treated for what turned out to be a fatal case of pneumonia? How old was Annabelle; where did she live? And what happened to her last name?*

It was mysterious, but probably not connected to the murders, Jessica decided. After all, according to the date on the chart, the woman had died nearly nine years ago. Annabelle S., whoever she was, was ancient history.

Jessica was about to replace the file when she heard something. What was that? She stood perfectly still, her ears pricked and her blood turning to ice in her veins. She heard it again, coming from the far end of the hall. A shutter rattling in the wind? Or a footstep?

Her heart in her throat, Jessica pushed the cabinet drawer shut. Sticking the Annabelle S. file in her shoulder bag, she leapt toward the door and then dashed on tiptoes down the hallway away from the scary noise.

Reaching the kitchen, she saw with relief that she'd left the window open. As she dove through it and landed on the damp earth below, Jessica was pretty sure she'd never been so glad to breathe the cold, misty London air.

The shuttered French doors opening out into Dr. Neville's side yard hadn't been too difficult to pry apart, using the tools she'd brought with her. Easing one of the doors open, Elizabeth stepped cautiously into the stale, musty air of the deserted apartment.

The dining room, she thought, taking another tentative step forward. The parquet floor creaked beneath her feet and she froze. What was that?

She thought she heard a distant creaking sound somewhere else on the ground floor of the house, like an echo of her own footsteps. Elizabeth listened, her heart thumping wildly. Silence.

"You're imagining things," she whispered to herself. "Nobody lives here anymore, and there's no such thing as ghosts."

However, on the off chance that she was wrong and the house was haunted by the unfortunate Dr. Neville and his gory throat, Elizabeth decided to make her tour as brief as possible.

I'm looking for a clue, something that might lead me to Robert, she reminded herself as she scurried down the hall past the doctor's waiting and examining rooms. *Maybe I can find out something about Neville, something that would have given Robert a reason to kill him.*

At the door to the doctor's study, Elizabeth paused, taking a moment to let her pulse slow and her thoughts untangle. As her eyes moved around the room, coming to rest on a row of filing cabinets, she had a peculiar sensation—like déjà vu, or the kind of tingle she got when her identical-twin intuition kicked in and she could almost feel her mind melding with Jessica's. The atmosphere of the room seemed charged with energy. *It's almost as if I've been here before,* Elizabeth thought, hugging herself to ward off a sudden chill. *But I haven't.*

She strode over to the file cabinets. The deceased physician's records were orderly and for the most part uninteresting. What was it about Neville, about Neville and Robert Pembroke Junior? Elizabeth wondered. Preposterous scenarios presented themselves as she flipped through the alphabetized patient files. Maybe Robert was a drug addict and came here to steal from Neville's pharmaceutical supply and Neville caught him at it and there was a scuffle. Maybe Robert knew something about Neville, or Neville knew something about Robert, or . . .

Spotting the Pembroke family files, Elizabeth plucked out Robert Junior's. It was fat; Neville had probably treated Robert since babyhood. "I'll take it home with me," Elizabeth murmured to herself. "Maybe a careful reading will turn up something useful."

Shutting the file cabinet drawer, she turned to the doctor's desk. A dark-green blotter, an old-fashioned brass pen-and-ink stand, and a small stack of monogrammed stationery stood at the ready, as if Dr. Neville might come in at any moment and sit down to jot a letter. Or make a phone call, Elizabeth thought, reaching for the Rolodex.

She thumbed through the cards. "Parker, Pease, Pembroke, Pitcairn," Elizabeth recited. "Player's Racquet Club, Plum's Pastry Shop, Portnoy, Price."

"Price!" she repeated, gaping at the card. "'Mildred Price, Pembroke nanny.'"

She nearly laughed as the inspiration struck. *I bet there's a lightbulb shining over my head, like in a comic strip! Yep, this could be it,* Elizabeth thought triumphantly. Little Bobby's old nanny. Where would you go if you were a spoiled young English lord deprived of hearth and home? Why, back to your doting nanny, of course!

Grabbing a pen and a piece of Dr. Neville's stationery, Elizabeth began to scribble down the nanny's address in Pelham. M-I-L-D-R-E-D P-R-I-C-E, she printed. Then her hand jerked and the pen skidded across the paper.

Something had startled her—a creak that sounded loud in the silent, empty flat. *Old houses make noises all by themselves,* Elizabeth reminded herself. *They shift and settle.* She stood perfectly still listening. Another creak, closer this time.

Old houses might shift and settle, but nevertheless Elizabeth had a sudden, overpowering feeling that someone . . . or something . . . was making the noise. She wasn't alone in Dr. Neville's apartment.

Leaving the half-written note, she ripped the card with Mildred Price's address from the Rolodex file and stuck it in her pocket. Racing to the doorway, she peered down the gloomy hall. Off to the right, Elizabeth heard another creak, sounding ominously like a foostep this time.

I don't believe in ghosts, I don't believe in ghosts, she chanted silently to herself as she dashed off to the left, heading at top speed for the dining room. Slipping back out into the side yard, she closed and shuttered the French door, and then leaned back against it for a moment, breathing hard.

Ghosts or no ghosts, she couldn't get out of that house fast enough . . . and she hoped she never had reason to come back again.

❖   ❖   ❖

38

The intruder prowled along the dim back hall of Dr. Neville's flat, his shoulders hunched, the muscles in his arms and legs tense. His breath came in ragged, painful gasps; tumultuous, unbearable emotions acted on his body like a whip, driving him, driving him mad. . . .

At the entrance to Dr. Neville's study, he paused. Clawing the door frame, he sniffed the air. Instantly, he recognized the scent of the two girls who had been there before him. A roar of outrage rumbled in his chest. He knew what brought them there. *They're looking for me. . . .*

Thoughts of the girls, and the hazy, nightmarish memory of what he'd done to Dr. Neville in that very house, lashed him into a frenzy. Leaping across the room, he yanked open the drawers of the file cabinet, one after another, frantically searching. *It's not here,* he realized at last, knocking over a cabinet in his haste and fury. *It's not here—they took it.*

An irresistible urge to destroy something, to rip it to pieces, swept over him, and a howl tore at his throat. Just as he raised an arm to sweep everything off the top of the desk, a scrap of paper caught his eye. He froze, staring at the name written there: Mildred Price.

Instantly, his fury dissolved and a look of cunning gleamed in his bloodshot eyes. *Nanny Millie,* he thought, crumpling the paper in his fist and stealing out of the room.

Chapter 3

Elizabeth checked her watch as she strode quickly away from Dr. Neville's. *Shoot,* she thought, seeing the time. She wanted to go to Pelham to talk with Mildred Price, but she'd made a date with Rene Glize to have tea. *It's already four—I'd better go straight to the restaurant,* she decided. *I can't stand him up again, after how he reacted last time!*

When Elizabeth and Jessica moved in at Housing for International Students, they'd been surprised and delighted to discover that Rene Glize, the young Frenchman they'd met on an exchange program to Cannes, was spending the summer in London and living at HIS, too. While she was in France, Elizabeth and Rene developed a special friendship bordering on romance, and meeting again in London, she'd felt immediately that the spark of attraction was still there. Clearly,

Rene thought so, too, and he'd rearranged his busy schedule at the French embassy so he would have time to take Elizabeth out to dinner.

But then she'd met Luke. The day of her dinner date with Rene, Elizabeth and Luke spent the afternoon sightseeing, and as afternoon melted into evening . . . and she grew increasingly captivated by Luke . . . she completely forgot about Rene. Offended and jealous, Rene had been cool to her for a week afterward, but he'd finally relented and they'd both agreed that the best course was just to be good friends.

It was always nice to hang out with Rene; still, as she rode the double-decker bus, Elizabeth could feel the Rolodex card burning a hole in her pocket. *The nanny will just have to wait until tomorrow,* she realized, swallowing her disappointment.

Rene was already seated at a table for two when Elizabeth arrived at the Parkview restaurant a few blocks from HIS. He stood up to pull out her chair. "I know it's terribly rude, but I had a cup of tea without you," he confessed. "This nasty English weather cuts right through to the bones. It is different from summer on the Riviera!"

Elizabeth laughed. "Tell me about it. Winter in southern California isn't this cold and damp!"

Rene filled Elizabeth's teacup. When a plate of fresh-baked scones and tiny tea sandwiches had been placed before them, he reached across the table to touch Elizabeth's hand. "I've been so busy at the embassy, we haven't had a chance to talk in days," he said. "I think about you all the time, though, and I worry about you. Ever since that horrible weekend you spent in the country, when the young woman was murdered in the very next room. . . ."

"So much has happened since then!" Elizabeth exclaimed. "You heard that young Lord Pembroke is the prime suspect?"

"Of course. No one talks of anything else."

"Well, this is how it came about. I was suspicious of Lord Pembroke Senior—I could tell he was hiding something, protecting somebody. So I went back to Pembroke Manor posing as Jessica. It turned out to be the very same day the cook, Maria—the one who'd gotten a glimpse of Joy Singleton's killer—was found murdered."

"You went back to Pembroke Manor?" Rene's dark eyebrows met in an anxious frown. "Why would you take such a risk?"

"I wanted to find out the truth about the Pembroke family. I wanted to learn their secrets."

"And you found . . . ?"

"All sorts of interesting things!" said Elizabeth. "When I was going through books in the library, I accidentally triggered a secret door that led into a little, hidden room full of books about werewolves and mounted animal heads and other creepy, superstitious things."

Rene gasped. "What does it mean?"

"I guess it means that the Pembrokes have a history of interest in werewolves. Pretty suggestive, considering the nature of the murders, wouldn't you say?"

"Umm," Rene agreed.

"Next I went upstairs to the room where Joy was murdered. I found a patch of fur and some dark-green silk threads snagged on the door frame—threads that turned out to be from Robert's bathrobe!"

"He went to the room that night—it was him!"

"It sure looks like it," agreed Elizabeth. "Right after that, I overheard Lord Pembroke speaking with Police Chief Thatcher and conceding that there was no other conclusion to reach. He realized he couldn't go on shielding his son—it would only lead to more bloodshed."

"But he must have warned Robert that the police were going to come after him, because Robert disappeared into thin air," said Rene.

"Right. And now he's out there somewhere. Someone attacked Jessica in the tube the other day, and I'm almost certain it was Robert. She doesn't want to believe she's in danger from him, though. That's why I'm going after Robert myself."

"I don't like you being so involved in this. I don't like it one bit. Until the killer is behind bars, you're not safe for one minute. Leave London, Elizabeth," Rene urged. "Go home to Sweet Valley."

A thrill of fear rippled through Elizabeth's body, but she dismissed Rene's earnest suggestion.

"We're only halfway through our internships at the *Journal*," she pointed out. "I don't know when I'll have another opportunity like this—I can't just throw it away."

"Then if nothing else, go to France and spend a few days with my mother," Rene persisted. He took Elizabeth's hand, squeezing it for emphasis. "She'd love to have you."

"You're sweet to be so concerned, but I'll be fine," Elizabeth assured him. She pressed his fingers, and then withdrew her hand. "Really." *Because I have Luke watching over me. . . .* "I'm not worried for myself, only for Jessica. After all, she's the one who's had two close calls at the hands—or should we say, paws?—of the wolfman!"

Rene's warnings were still ringing in Elizabeth's ears as she returned to HIS half an hour later. *Until the killer is behind bars, you're not safe . . . leave London . . . go home . .* It was a chill, rainy dusk; Elizabeth found herself looking over her shoulder as she passed the park. *Why did I insist that I didn't mind walking home alone?* she wondered, wishing she'd taken Rene up on his offer to escort her to the dorm before heading into town for an embassy function. *I could've let him do that much for me.*

With a surge of relief, she reached the gate at HIS and ran up the steps. With lights twinkling at every window, the brick Georgian boardinghouse looked cozy and warm. *With Mrs. Bates keeping us under lock and key, we couldn't be safer,* Elizabeth thought as she took the stairs to the third floor two at a time.

The bedroom she and Jessica shared with Portia, and formerly Lina as well, was empty. Dropping her jacket and purse on a chair, Elizabeth spotted a folded note card on her dressing table. "Liz," Portia had written in her distinctive, flowery script, "I've gone with Jessica, Emily, and Gabriello to hear G's friend Basil's band. Join us at the Star Twenty Club if you like. Love, P."

Elizabeth felt a pang of regret. Lunar Landscape was a fun dance band—the gang had seen them play before. *But maybe it's just as well I wasn't around when they headed out,* she thought, tossing the note in the wastebasket. *It would've been awkward, since Jessica and I aren't talking. . . .*

Anyway, she had work to do. Curling up in one of the easy chairs, she opened up Robert's medical file. She went through it page by page, reading every single word. There were records of Robert's childhood vaccines and annual checkups, charts relating to a tonsillectomy at age eight, and write-ups of visits over the years for strep throat, the flu, a broken arm after a fall from a horse, stitches in his knee, the flu again.

What a letdown, Elizabeth thought, closing the folder with a sigh. Robert had been a typically healthy, if somewhat accident-prone, boy. The file revealed nothing.

Tucking up her legs, she hugged her knees. The room seemed too quiet; she was lonely for someone to talk to. *If only Lina were still around,* Elizabeth thought. *Maybe I'll call Luke, just to chat.* She got to her feet, only to remember that she didn't have Luke's home telephone number. *Funny he never gave it to me. . . .* But maybe not; because they saw each other every day at the *Journal,* she really had no need for it. And besides, she'd gotten the distinct impression that Luke's home life with his widowed father was far from happy. *He just doesn't want to open that up to me. That's OK—he's entitled.*

Elizabeth sighed heavily, thinking about how easy it would be to pick up the phone and call one of her friends if she were home in Sweet Valley. Enid or Penny or Olivia or DeeDee . . . or Todd.

Crossing the room, Elizabeth opened her top dresser drawer. After hiding the medical file under a pile of clothes, she took out her most recent letter from Todd. Returning to the chair, she sat down again, wrapping one of Mrs. Bates's crocheted afghans around her legs.

The letter was newsy and affectionate. Todd hadn't known anything about the werewolf killings when he wrote it; neither had he known, and he still didn't, that she'd met another boy.

As she reread the letter, losing herself in memories of Sweet Valley and Todd, Elizabeth gradually pushed all thoughts of Luke and Rene and the

47

newspaper and the Pembrokes and the murders from her mind. She laughed at his humorous account of a pool party at Ken Matthews', and sniffled when he wrote of haunting the mailbox in hopes of receiving a letter or postcard from England.

A painful feeling of homesickness rushed over her. Suddenly, Elizabeth found herself missing the bright stucco houses on Calico Drive, the warm southern California sunshine. She missed the beach and the ocean, and her parents, and her older brother, Steven, and his girlfriend, Billy, and Prince Albert, the family's golden retriever. *And Todd,* Elizabeth thought, her heart aching. *I miss Todd.*

It was the first time since she'd been in London that she'd really and truly felt that. There'd been so many distractions, so much excitement, and developing a wild crush on Luke Shepherd hadn't left her much time to think about Todd. But as a soft London rain pattered against the windows, Elizabeth realized something, felt something deep in her heart. *England is a foreign land. No matter how crazy I am about Luke, we're from different worlds. He could never replace Todd.*

Still, on a cold, gray, lonely night like this, Elizabeth would have been happy to feel Luke's strong arms wrapping around her. She grew warm just thinking about their first passionate kiss, in the woods of the Pembroke estate. The first of many such kisses . . .

"Under the circumstances, I'm pretty lucky to

have him," Elizabeth said out loud, fingering the silver pendant. "Because of him, I'm never really alone."

Unclasping the pendant, Elizabeth studied its strange, mystical markings: the head of a sharp-fanged wolf in a five-pointed star. Turning it over, she noticed for the first time that the initial "A" was engraved on the back. *Luke never told me where this came from—I wonder if it belonged to his mother?*

She knew how much Luke still missed the mother who had died when he was only eight years old, knew he still mourned. It was a sign of how much Elizabeth meant to him that Luke had entrusted the precious necklace to her.

Maybe it is magical, Elizabeth thought. *Nothing bad has happened to me since I've been wearing it. But do I really need it, when I have Luke to protect me? Isn't it selfish to keep it to myself when Jessica is so much more vulnerable?*

The shoulder bag Jessica carried to work was slung over the post of their bunk bed. Unzipping the inside pocket, Elizabeth tucked the pendant underneath a powder compact and a couple of lipsticks. It seemed like a small, insignificant gesture compared to the threat that loomed over them. Maybe it wouldn't help . . . but it couldn't hurt.

"The band is hot tonight," Emily raved, joining Jessica on the sidelines of the dance floor at the

Star Twenty Club, an underage juice bar. "How come you're not out there?"

Jessica shrugged. "There's nobody to dance with."

Emily laughed. "Are you joking? This place is crawling with gorgeous guys. Don't tell me none of them have approached you."

Jessica shrugged again. "I guess I'm just not in the mood."

"Well, let's sit down for a minute, then," suggested Emily. "Here comes Portia now."

After buying soft drinks at the bar, the three girls retreated to a relatively quiet corner. "What's on your mind?" Portia asked Jessica.

Jessica sighed. "What do you think?"

"Robert." Portia gave Jessica's hand a sympathetic pat. "I know this is tough on you. You must really miss him."

"I do," Jessica confessed, her eyes smarting with unshed tears. "But I'm taking your advice—I'm not just sitting around." Quickly, she related her afternoon adventure at Dr. Neville's boarded-up flat. "It was kind of a random search," she admitted, "seeing as how I had no idea what I was looking for. And the place was so creepy—I was practically jumping out of my skin the entire time. The only thing I came out with was this file. . . ."

She told the other girls about the Annabelle S. file, currently hidden under her mattress at HIS. Emily and Portia were intrigued. "It's so mysterious," exclaimed Emily. "Who could she have been?"

Portia rubbed her hands together. "I'm sure there's something illicit about it," she declared enthusiastically. "There are all sorts of old books and movies with titles like 'The True Story of Madame D.' They're usually pretty racy—the person's identity is hidden because she's having an adulterous affair or something like that."

"An affair?" Jessica wrinkled her nose. "With old Dr. Neville? He must have been sixty."

"Well, he wasn't always sixty," Portia pointed out, "and didn't you say it was an old file?"

"That's right," said Emily. "Annabelle S. died years ago—maybe they had a clandestine romance when they were young."

"Or maybe Annabelle S. had an affair with someone else, but Dr. Neville knew about it and was protecting him," suggested Portia.

Jessica nodded slowly, thinking back to the morning after Dr. Neville's murder when she and Elizabeth peeked through the window and saw the police chief and Lord Pembroke standing over the body. "Robert told me that Neville was his father's best friend," said Jessica. "Maybe the file will turn out to be helpful after all. Maybe there's some connection between the Pembrokes and Annabelle S.!"

"Let's pick up the pace," suggested Gabriello. "It's nearly eleven—curfew. We don't want Mrs. Bates to lock us out."

The four teenagers trudged quickly along the deserted street. Fog blanketed the city; the mist-shrouded streetlights offered little illumination. "Whose idea was it to walk, anyway?" muttered Emily. "We can't see two feet in front of our noses. What if we get lost?"

"We won't get lost," Portia assured her. "The club is only six blocks from HIS—it would have been silly to take a taxi. Don't be such a scaredy-cat!"

We won't get lost . . . don't be such a scaredy-cat. . . . Her hands pushed deep in the pockets of her jacket, Jessica walked as fast as she could. She repeated the words silently to herself, trying to feel as fearless as Portia sounded. *We won't get lost . . . don't be such a scaredy-cat. . . .*

"This reminds me of Lina and Elizabeth's story, the night we all went to hear the band at Mondo and those two left early and walked home alone," said Emily, her teeth chattering. "Remember? They got lost in the fog and stumbled upon the body of that dead dog."

Jessica's skin crawled. The werewolf got Poo-Poo that night. And he'd be out on a night like this. . . .

From the start, Jessica had laughed off Elizabeth's werewolf warnings, accusing her sister of having an out-of-control hyperactive imagination. But the attack in the tube station was still fresh in Jessica's mind. She vividly recalled the ominous sound of footsteps behind her, something panting loudly, a hairy arm brushing against hers. . . .

Jessica glanced apprehensively over her shoulder. The mist swirled all around them, thick and ghostly-white and impenetrable. *Someone—something—could be following us right now, but we wouldn't even know it.* She thought about the spooky noises she'd heard that afternoon in Dr. Neville's supposedly empty apartment and her heart galloped. *Following us . . . following me.*

She stepped closer to Gabriello, taking comfort in his rangy, athletic physique and confident stride. *There's safety in numbers . . . isn't there? The werewolf wouldn't attack four people at once . . . would he?*

"Winchester Street!" Emily cried with audible relief as they came to an intersection. "We're almost home."

Her friends hadn't wanted to admit they'd been scared, so no one could admit how glad they were to see the lights of HIS. But as they practically sprinted up the front steps, just as Mrs. Bates was peering out into the dark prior to bolting the front door, Jessica could tell she wasn't the only one whose heart was hammering.

"It's five minutes past eleven," Mrs. Bates informed them in a chiding tone. "You're right lucky my evening telly program ran late. Now hustle inside, the lot of you!"

Jessica and the others piled into the warm, brightly lit front hallway. Suddenly, Portia, Emily, and Gabriello were all smiling and chattering again, relief oozing out of their very pores. As Mrs. Bates double-bolted the door, Jessica leaned against the wall, taking deep breaths to calm her racing pulse. She couldn't wait to crawl into bed— she wished she could go to sleep for a week.

How many more nights like this? she wondered, not sure she could endure many more. *How many more scary, lonely nights? Will the police catch the werewolf before he strikes again? Will Robert ever come back to me?*

Chapter 4

After finishing breakfast on Monday morning, Elizabeth and Emily carried their dishes to the HIS kitchen. "Ready to go?" Emily asked. "I'll walk out with you."

"Actually . . ." Elizabeth glanced back into the dining room, which was fast emptying out. Portia had just come down for her morning coffee, still rumpled and sleepy, but everyone else had eaten and was leaving for work or school. *Everyone but Jessica,* Elizabeth noticed. *She's oversleeping, for a change.* "I think I might have another cup of tea. You go on ahead."

"Right-o," Emily said cheerfully. "See you to-night!"

Elizabeth loitered by the buffet table, looking from her wristwatch to the teapot and back again. *Should I run upstairs and wake her?* she wondered. As annoyed as she was with her sister, Elizabeth didn't like the idea of Jessica taking the tube to work by herself. *Come to think of it, I don't want to go alone, either!*

At the same time . . . Elizabeth picked up a clean teacup, then put it down again. *If I wait for her, I'll just be late myself. Jessica is responsible for getting herself up and out of here—I'm not her alarm clock.*

Waving good-bye to Portia, Elizabeth headed into the foyer and out the door. Overhead, the morning sun fought to break through a bank of low, iron-gray clouds. A cool breeze fingered Elizabeth's hair as she stepped through the HIS gate onto the sidewalk.

Her eyes fixed straight ahead, Elizabeth walked quickly down the street toward the tube station. After a block, she came abreast of the park where she and Luke had walked together . . . and kissed . . . Friday evening.

Usually, she and Jessica were part of a steady stream of people walking to work, but this morning, Elizabeth found she had the sidewalk to herself. *I'm glad I'm out in the open and it's daylight,* she thought, stepping up her pace. *I just hope there are more people in the tube station. I don't want to be alone there, like Jessica the other day . . . like Jessica . . . like Jessica. . . .*

Suddenly, the hair on the back of Elizabeth's neck stood on end. She felt electrified, as if she'd

56

just stuck her finger in a light socket. She felt naked, exposed. She felt a pair of eyes staring at her, staring hard.

Someone's following me, she realized, the certainty hitting her with the force of a lightning bolt. *The pendant. Oh, why did I take off the pendant?*

She stopped in her tracks, her breath coming fast. Slowly, she pivoted on one heel to look back, afraid of what she might see . . . of what she might not see.

A tall, dark-haired young man in a dark suit and sunglasses was walking nearly a block behind her. When she stopped and turned, he veered abruptly off to the side, striding quickly into the wooded park, his face turned away from her. Once again, the sidewalk was deserted.

Elizabeth hunched her shoulders, shivering. From a distance, and with the shadows of the trees, she hadn't been able to tell if it was anyone she knew. Robert Pembroke had dark hair, but for that matter, so did lots of people, including Rene and Luke. She stood for a moment, waiting to see if the man would reappear. When he didn't, she darted across the intersection and continued on the other side of the street.

Just somebody going to work, taking a shortcut through the park, she told herself. *It wasn't the wolfman. Did it look like the wolfman? Hardly!*

Still berating herself for being paranoid, Elizabeth reached the entrance to the underground train station. She walked right by it, joining the queue at the bus stop instead. *It's not as fast,* she figured. *I'll have to switch buses and then walk a few extra blocks.* But this morning, that suited Elizabeth just fine. *There's no way I'm taking the tube!*

Jessica sat up in bed, rubbing her eyes. "I hate getting up for work. I hate Mondays," she groaned. She especially hated getting up this morning, because she'd barely slept a wink—she'd tossed and turned restlessly all night.

It must be late, she thought, gazing tiredly around the empty bedroom. Even Portia was out of bed. Jessica focused on the clock and grimaced. *It is late. It's really late!*

For a moment, Jessica felt a brief pang for the old days at home in Sweet Valley. *Liz would always wake me up when I overslept on schooldays,* she remembered nostalgically. *She'd yell, or throw something at me—she'd threaten to take the Jeep and leave me behind.*

With a sigh, Jessica hopped out of bed. Reaching into the closet, she grabbed the first shirt and skirt her hands touched. She didn't care how she looked; she didn't even care if her outfit matched.

She dressed quickly. Leaving her bed rumpled, she stuck her arms in the sleeves of her navy blazer and ran down the hall, stopping in the bathroom to brush her teeth and splash water on her face.

"Ugh," she muttered, staring at her pale face in the mirror. "You need makeup in a major way, Wakefield."

But there really wasn't time. Hurrying downstairs, Jessica bypassed the dining room, with its tempting smell of fresh-baked scones, and headed straight out to the sidewalk.

Halfway to the tube station, she reached for her wallet to buy a piece of fruit from a sidewalk vendor and made a discovery. "Darn!" she exclaimed, stomping her foot in aggravation. "I left my dumb bag with my dumb wallet and mini-corder and notebook back at the dumb dorm. Grrr!"

Wheeling, she jogged back toward HIS. *It's starting out to be another great day*, she thought sarcastically. *I look hideous, I feel worse, I'm late for work. Oh, yeah, and the whole United Kingdom thinks my boyfriend is a werewolf.*

Inside the dorm, she took the stairs to the top floor three at a time. *That's funny*, she thought as she approached her room. The door was slightly ajar—she usually closed it. *But then, if I could forget my purse, I could forget that, too.*

Reaching the end of the hallway, she stepped into her room and then froze, her eyes widening. "Somebody's been here," she gasped. "Robert. Robert was here!"

She clutched the back of a chair, her knees turning to butter. Since she left just a short time ago, Robert had been in her room, she was sure of

59

it. She could smell his cologne, just a faint wisp of it, teasing her senses; she could feel the magnetism of his presence. "And my bed—someone made my bed."

She rushed over to touch the neatly smoothed coverlet on her bunk. "He was here," she repeated, her eyes lighting up. "He came to see me!"

Joy and love and hope flooded Jessica's heart, like the morning sun bursting through the clouds after a stormy night. Robert hadn't forsaken her, hadn't forgotten her; he'd risked his freedom to come to her. He'd been right there, where she stood, and only moments before—he must have left right before she returned.

Her shoulder bag was draped over the bunk post. Grabbing it, Jessica tore back down the hallway and downstairs. Her heart pounding, she flung open the door and raced to the gate, eagerly looking both ways. "Robert!" she cried.

He'd been there, but now he was gone. The streets were empty; there was no one in sight but a bedraggled, stubble-faced homeless man in a patched brown coat with a battered felt hat pulled down low on his forehead, poking around in a trash can with a stick.

Jessica stared at the homeless man, her eyes welling up with tears. Her hopes had soared so high; now the disappointment struck her like a blow. "Robert," she whispered, sinking down onto the curb. "Robert."

The tears spilled from her eyes, pouring down both cheeks. Sitting on the curb with her arms wrapped around her knees, Jessica buried her head and sobbed.

Striding into the busy offices of the *London Journal*, Elizabeth waved at the people she knew, calling hello. "Good morning, Rebecca. Hi, Arthur. Hi, Zena. Hello—"

Halfway across the newsroom, Elizabeth skidded to a stop abreast of the editor-in-chief's office. The massive, walnut desk had been empty for a few days, since the firing of Henry Reeves, but now someone was sitting there.

Elizabeth blinked in disbelief at the lovely, chestnut-haired woman. "Lucy? Is that you?"

Lucy Friday waved carelessly at the new brass nameplate on the door. "It's me," she confirmed, pushing her tortoiseshell glasses up on her aristocratic nose. "I'm back."

Elizabeth gaped at the nameplate. "Lucy Friday, editor-in-chief!" she read out loud. "But how—when—" She stuttered to a stop.

Lucy laughed. "Close your mouth, Elizabeth," she advised cheerfully. "You look like a fish on a hook. That's better. Now, turn around and toddle on back to the newsroom. I'm about to call my first staff meeting—you shouldn't miss it."

Clapping her hands and whistling, Lucy soon had the entire *London Journal* staff assembled.

Across the newsroom, Elizabeth spotted Luke and his boss, Martha, the arts editor. She waved at Luke and at her own boss, Tony Frank, who'd been promoted from society editor to take over the crime desk vacated by Lucy.

"This will be short and sweet," Lucy promised, leaning back against a desk with her slender ankles crossed. "You already know me, so I don't have to introduce myself, and you know my style. Well, my style," she said with a smile, "is now the style of the whole newspaper. In a few words: high-energy, no-nonsense. Aim high and get the job done. Now, we've all been concerned about competition lately. This is the bottom line on that subject. The *London Journal* is a newspaper, not a scandal sheet. We will not compete with the *London Daily Post* by imitating the *London Daily Post*. We will compete with them—and we will outsell them—by presenting more real news in greater depth. Got that?"

Her reply was an enthusiastic standing ovation. "One last thing before we all get back to work," Lucy said. "I need your cooperation on the werewolf murder case. If any of you becomes privy to any information, come to me immediately. Serial killers often make contact with the press, even develop a dialogue with an individual reporter—they're crying out for attention. The smallest tidbit could lead to a big breakthrough for Scotland Yard, so let's keep our eyes open and our ears peeled. Thanks for your time."

The meeting broke up. As Elizabeth followed Tony back to his desk, she saw to her surprise that Lucy was doing the same thing. Elizabeth hung back, letting the editor-in-chief approach the crime desk first. "Frank," Lucy said, rapping briskly on the wall of his cubicle. "May I have a word?"

Tony grinned. "A word? You may have ten thousand words, Miss Friday. Talk all day, if you'd like. Your voice is music to my ears."

"Cut the baloney," Lucy advised. "I'm here on business, Frank."

"Er, of course. I understand that now—you're in charge, and—can't joke around like we used to—"

"Like *you* used to," Lucy corrected. "This is the deal, Frank. You're free to joke all you want on your own time. But I'm not giving anything away here. Reeves made you the temporary crime editor and the assignment's still temporary. I want to see for myself what you can do."

Tony raised his sandy-blond eyebrows. "You mean, I'm on trial?"

"Let's just say that if someone better comes along, you may find yourself back on the society page." Lucy tipped her head thoughtfully. "Now, I like that Adam Silver who covers crime for the *Daily Post*. He's one of their better people—a real go-getter."

Tony frowned. "Silver's nothing but an ambulance chaser."

"And a darned good one," said Lucy. "He never gets caught flat-footed."

With that, Lucy sailed off. Elizabeth stared after her and then turned back to Tony. She expected him to be crestfallen. Instead, Tony tipped back in his chair with his feet on the desk, a broad grin wreathing his face. "I say, isn't it fitting? Isn't it grand? Just like a Hollywood movie. Noble, high-minded Lucy resigns her post as crime editor to protest Reeves suppressing the facts about Dr. Neville's gruesome murder. She's ready to sacrifice her career rather than be party to a cover-up. We investigative reporters take a pledge," he told Elizabeth, lifting one hand dramatically, "to tell the whole truth and nothing but the truth!"

"I remember all that," said Elizabeth. "But how did Lucy get to be the new editor-in-chief?"

"Well, it turns out our gal Friday was right, of course, and the *Journal's* owner, Lord Pembroke himself, was behind the decision to downplay the murders. He was protecting his son, we now know. But he never authorized Reeves to print lies. Reeves went too far, printing the unsubstantiated rumor about Princess Eliana's corpse turning up. In his misguided effort to one-up the *Daily Post*, he disgraced the *Journal* and himself."

"Yeah, yeah, I was here for that part, too," Elizabeth exclaimed somewhat impatiently.

"Well, the rest is simple. Pembroke fired Reeves, and he hired back Lucy in his place."

"What a vindication for Lucy!"

"Isn't it capital for her?" Tony agreed. "Though

now she's the big cheese, she's less likely than ever to give me the time of day." He sighed regretfully. "But what a stroke of genius on Pembroke's part! He's been worried about competition from the *Daily Post*? Why, under the stewardship of Lucy Friday, the *London Journal* will . . ."

Elizabeth suspected Tony's rhapsodic monologue could go on all day. Leaving Tony droning on to himself, she ducked out to visit Luke.

The arts and entertainment staff had desks in the far corner of the newsroom, around a bend in the hallway. "So, what's your opinion of our new editor-in-chief?" Luke asked, rising to give Elizabeth a quick hug.

Elizabeth blushed, glad there was no one else around to see them. "I think it's great. You should see Tony—he's delirious."

"He had her on a pretty lofty pedestal before," Luke remarked. "Now he'll probably place her so high, she'll be lost in the clouds."

"He has the hugest crush on her," Elizabeth agreed. "And for all her hands-off attitude, I think Lucy's hot for him, too. They just don't seem to get it. It's obvious to everybody else they're meant for each other—why can't they figure it out?"

"People can be pretty dense when it comes to matters of the heart. As for those two, I think they're too busy pretending the only thing they care about is getting the story," guessed Luke. "Reporters are supposed to be cynical and hard-nosed and detached, not sentimental and romantic." He put his arms around her again and nuzzled her neck. "Lucky for me, I'm a poet. I'm not afraid to follow my feelings, wherever they might lead me."

Elizabeth closed her eyes, melting as Luke kissed her throat, then her cheeks, then her lips. "Umm," she murmured. "But Lucy and Tony might have a point. This isn't necessarily the best way to get in the mood to write up the latest London crime story!"

Luke chuckled. Stepping back, he held her at arm's length, his blue eyes twinkling. "Sorry. I got carried away. It seems to happen all the time when I'm around you."

Elizabeth smiled, a tiny dimple creasing her left cheek. "Good thing we work at opposite ends of the newsroom."

At that moment, Luke's gaze dropped from Elizabeth's face to her neck, and his smile faded. "Elizabeth!" Reaching out, he touched her bare skin with one fingertip. "The pendant. You're not wearing it."

Elizabeth put a hand to her throat, remembering how naked and vulnerable she'd felt on her way to work, when she thought someone was following her. *I can't tell Luke about that—he'd only worry more.* "I gave it to Jessica," she explained, her tone carefree and light. "She needs it more than I do."

Luke frowned. "But you could be in danger,

too, Elizabeth—no less than Jessica. The only reason I'm able to sleep at night is knowing you're wearing the pendant—that you're shielded, safe."

"You take such good care of me yourself," said Elizabeth. "The pendant can't do nearly as much for me."

Luke folded her in his arms, resting his chin on top of her head. "I'm trying to take care of you. I'm trying."

Elizabeth pressed her face against his firm chest. She wondered if Jessica had found the pendant in her shoulder bag yet—if she was wearing it. "That reminds me," she said out loud. She knew it was painful for Luke to talk about his mother, but she was too curious not to ask. "When I took off the necklace, I noticed the letter 'A' etched on the back. Was that your mother's initial?"

"Yes." Luke's breath was soft and warm on her hair, his tone sad. "Her name was Ann. The pendant belonged to her. As I've mentioned, she was fascinated with werewolf lore."

"It's a very special keepsake, then. Jessica will take good care of it, don't worry."

At that moment, they heard footsteps pounding down the hall in their direction. They jumped apart guiltily just as Tony Frank careened around the corner.

Tony's sandy hair stood on end and his eyes glittered. *Something's up*, Elizabeth guessed, her pulse accelerating.

67

"There you are, Liz!" Tony exclaimed. "I just got a call about a murder in Pelham. Details are sketchy, but it could be the werewolf again. Here's our chance to prove ourselves to the boss. Let's hop to!"

A murder in Pelham! Elizabeth thought, adrenaline coursing through her veins. She climbed into the roomy backseat of the taxi and Tony followed suit after barking the address at the driver. "And make it fast!" Elizabeth heard her boss holler.

The cabbie dove into the driver's seat and gunned the engine. The big black Austin shot out into traffic. "Pelham," Elizabeth said, turning to Tony. "That's where the Pembrokes' old nanny lives!"

"Hmm." Tony looked up from the notebook he'd been flipping through energetically. "What, the Pembrokes' nanny, you say? Do we have any interest in her?"

"Possibly." Elizabeth hesitated for an instant, and then confessed that she'd broken into Dr. Neville's flat the previous afternoon. "Who could know the family members better than someone who lived with them for years?" Elizabeth asked. "The nanny may have information about Robert's whereabouts—she may even have seen him!"

"True. True!" Tony declared.

"I was planning to visit her at some point today. So, as long as we're in the neighborhood anyway . . ."

"We can swing by her house on the way back from this case," Tony proposed. "You're right, Liz—the nanny could be a good lead." His eyes twinkled. "Of course, I can't officially approve of your methods, but off the record: jolly good work!"

The cabbie continued to speed through town, weaving expertly in and out of traffic. At the outskirts of the city, the traffic thinned. The taxi roared along so fast, it almost overshot the turn. "Whoa, here's our road!" Tony shouted.

The driver slammed on the brakes and yanked the steering wheel. Tires squealing, they swung onto a side street.

Elizabeth glanced at the road sign, and then did a double take. "Bishop Street," she squeaked in surprise.

"Umm, yes," Tony mumbled, once again poring over the notes he'd taken when the call about the murder came through to the paper.

Bishop Street . . . Elizabeth's heart began to thump madly in her chest. According to the Rolodex card she'd filched from Dr. Neville's office, Mildred Price, the Pembrokes' former nanny, lived on Bishop Street. *It's a coincidence—just a coincidence,* Elizabeth told herself. But suddenly her mouth was dry as dust.

Elizabeth looked at the houses passing by, her eyes searching for street numbers. Eighteen, twenty-two, twenty-nine . . . "T–T–Tony," she stuttered, a feeling of dread tying her tongue in a knot.

"Where are we going? Where did the murder take place?"

At that moment, the cabbie braked in front of an ivy-covered cobblestone cottage. An ambulance was parked just ahead; two police cars flanked the ambulance, lights flashing and sirens wailing.

Elizabeth knew what Tony was going to say before he said it. "Thirty-seven Bishop Street," he told her, reaching for the door handle. "And here we are!"

The Rolodex card was tucked inside Elizabeth's wallet, but now she saw it as clearly as if she held it in front of her eyes. "Mildred Price, 37 Bishop Street, Pelham . . ."

A van from a local television station tore down the road, pulling over next to the taxi. As Tony and Elizabeth hurried toward the cottage gate, Tony gestured toward a beat-up green Triumph sports car parked in front of the house next door. "What did I tell you about ambulance chasing? It's Silver," he said wryly. "Can't say the *London Daily Post* doesn't know how to sniff out a story!"

The TV reporters, Adam Silver, and a police officer were talking to a young woman standing on the front lawn. Another police officer helped the ambulance crew wheel a gurney down the walk.

The blood drained from Elizabeth's face. She witnessed it all as if from a distance; the roaring in her ears deafened her. *No*, she thought. *Not her, too. Not her.*

But she'd seen the name on the picket fence. Price, #37.

"It's the nanny, Mildred Price," Elizabeth whispered.

Tony gaped at her, and then at the sheet-draped corpse on the gurney. "The nanny? Mildred Price was the Pembrokes' nanny?" Tony waved to Adam Silver of the *Daily Post*. "Silver, have they confirmed the identity of the victim?"

The *Daily Post's* crackerjack crime reporter stepped to Tony's side. "Yep, it's the old woman, Mrs. Price—she lived here alone." Silver's icy gray eyes glittered in much the same way Tony's had when he'd come to Elizabeth in the office to sweep her off to investigate. *It's a story,* she thought dully. *To them, it's just a good story.*

"Foul play, no doubt about it," Silver continued. "I caught a glimpse of the body before they covered it."

Elizabeth stared at the still, white-shrouded form being lifted into the back of the ambulance.

"Her throat was horribly mangled," related Silver. "Ripped right open. Beastly."

Beastly . . . "The werewolf," Elizabeth gasped.

Chapter 5

"The werewolf," repeated Adam Silver, his eyes fixed on Elizabeth's pale, shocked face. "It certainly looks like it, doesn't it? The brutally torn throat seems to be our serial killer's personal signature. But why this victim? Why a harmless white-haired old widow lady?"

Turning away from the *Daily Post* reporter, Elizabeth choked back a sob. Silver paced off again to badger a policeman for more information.

Tony stepped closer to Elizabeth and put a hand on her shoulder. "Are you all right?" he asked gently.

Elizabeth shook her head. The tears she'd been fighting to hold back squeezed out. "Robert was here," she cried, wiping her damp cheek on her sleeve. "He did stop by to see his old nanny—to kill her. If only I'd come straight over here yesterday! I could have talked to her. I could have warned her. She might still be alive, instead of . . . instead of . . ."

Another sob wracked Elizabeth's body. "It's silly to blame yourself," insisted Tony. His grip on her shoulder tightening, he gave her a little shake. "If Robert was bent on knocking her off, he'd have found a way, no matter what. And chances are, old Mrs. Price wouldn't have believed you, anyway. She wouldn't have believed that her dear little boy could intend her or anyone else any harm."

Elizabeth nodded, trying to find comfort in Tony's reasoning. Tony turned on his heel to watch as Adam Silver hopped into his Triumph and roared off in a cloud of exhaust. A grim smile twisted his lips. "He thinks he has the scoop," Tony said with satisfaction. "He doesn't know the Pembroke connection, though—we've got him there! Lucy'll be proud of us."

Elizabeth took a tissue from her purse and blew her nose. "Robert Pembroke is the killer, isn't he?" she said quietly. "This clinches it."

"He's incriminated more than ever," Tony agreed.

Elizabeth tried to picture Robert in a murderous rage, attacking an innocent old woman who loved him—whom he himself had once loved. *I guess to a killer, no one is sacred. No one is safe. So, what about Jessica?* Elizabeth thought. *Will the pendant help her if Robert goes after her next?*

"He has to be stopped," she said out loud. "But how? What if the police can't catch him? Where will the bloodshed end?"

"Here's the research you wanted about the airline merger," Jessica said, stepping into Lucy Friday's new office and waving a fat manila folder.

"Jessica, you're a whiz," Lucy declared, taking the folder and glancing quickly at its contents. "I thought you'd need all day to get this together."

Jessica shrugged. "It's a trick I learned at school. When you have work to do, do it fast. Then you can go to the beach or the mall."

Lucy laughed. "I like your style, Wakefield. Fast is fine with me, as long as you also do your work well."

"I was pretty thorough," Jessica promised.

"Super." Lucy dropped the folder onto her desk and sat back down. "Well, I suppose now I have to turn you back over to Frank."

Jessica thought she detected a note of reluctance in Lucy's matter-of-fact voice. *Go for it,* she commanded herself. "Lucy, I mean, Miss Friday, I mean Miss Editor-in-Chief . . ."

Lucy waved away Jessica's fumbling attempts at propriety. "Lucy will do."

"Lucy, Tony's off on some story with Elizabeth and I—" Jessica gestured to the manila folder. "I'd rather do stuff for you," she announced boldly. "In your new job, you'll probably need a lot of extra help. You should definitely have your own summer intern. Can I be it?"

Lucy drummed her fingers on the desk, a thoughtful smile on her lips. "My own intern, eh? It would be handy having one." She narrowed her eyes at Jessica. "But I thought you and your sister were inseparable. A package deal, Tony told me on your first day here. If you work for me, this won't be as fun for you—you won't see much of Elizabeth."

"That's the way I want it," Jessica confessed. "Liz and I aren't getting along these days. In fact, we're not speaking to each other, which makes it kind of hard to work together. I don't want to be around her, but if Tony's my boss I can't avoid her."

Lucy continued to drum her fingers, pondering the proposal. Jessica held her breath. "Well, Wakefield," Lucy said at last, "I can't say I blame you for wanting a change from that society editor in crime editor's clothing. Frank is a lightweight. You'll learn more from me."

Jessica's eyes lit up. "You mean I can be your intern?"

"I'll be glad to have your help," Lucy assented.

"That's great," Jessica gushed, sitting down across the desk from the editor-in-chief, her new boss. "Oh, you've made my day!"

"But I have some advice for you."

"What's that?"

"Ordinarily, I wouldn't stick my nose into a colleague's personal business. I feel strongly that we should keep our private lives private—in other words, out of the office. But since you brought it up . . . it's no good fighting with your sister, Wakefield."

"She started it," Jessica protested. "She's being impossible. And cruel." Tears stung her eyes, but she blinked them back, refusing to cry in front of Lucy. "She wants Robert to be found guilty. She won't admit that the evidence could point in a whole bunch of different directions. She doesn't care about my feelings at all."

Reaching across the desk, Lucy placed her hand briefly on Jessica's. "No doubt about it, young Rob Pembroke is in a tough spot. It's dreadful for you if you care about him. But you two girls mustn't feud. Take it from me—I know. I have a sister of my own who's just as hardheaded and stubborn as I am, but even when we have a row, I never forget that she's my best friend."

"Elizabeth isn't my friend," Jessica insisted. "Not anymore."

"Blood is thicker than water," Lucy countered. "We'll find a way to patch things up between the two of you. In the meantime, let's check the storyboard, shall we?"

Jessica trooped after Lucy, her lips pressed together in a tight line. *Lucy thinks she's made up her mind, but I made my mind up first.* Jessica intended to work like a dog as Lucy's intern: run any errand, research any story, do anything Lucy asked her. Anything, that is, but kiss and make up with Elizabeth.

When the gurney was loaded into the ambulance, the attendant pulled the doors shut. As Elizabeth and Tony watched, the ambulance driver hit the gas, speeding off down Bishop Street with the siren blaring.

"Let's get some details, Elizabeth," said Tony. "I want to talk to the person who found the body."

They walked up the flagstone path to the front door of the cottage. Colorful flower beds bordered the path, and neatly pruned rosebushes laden with fragrant blossoms clustered under the cottage's front windows. Elizabeth sniffled, imagining the kindly old woman tending her garden in days past. *Poor old Mrs. Price. Who will give her flowers such loving care now?*

After examining Tony's press card, the police officer standing at the door waved them in, pointing to a small parlor off the front hall. "The victim's granddaughter is in there, Dolores Price," the officer said. "She's the one who discovered the body and called us over."

A young woman in her early twenties with curly auburn hair and a tear-streaked face sat on an overstuffed sofa, staring at the telephone on the end table. When Tony cleared his throat, she looked up with glazed eyes. "I have to phone the rest of the family . . . her friends," Dolores stammered tearfully. "Oh, I just can't bear to!"

Elizabeth sat down next to Dolores and patted her arm helplessly. Tony took a notebook and pen from his jacket pocket. "Miss Price, I know you're upset—very understandably so. You have our sincere sympathy, and our apologies for intruding on your grief like this. But would you take a few minutes to speak with us?"

Dolores nodded. "Poor Gran," she whispered. "There's nothing I can do for her now but tell her story."

"According to the police, you found the body," stated Tony. Unobtrusively, Elizabeth removed her mini-corder from her purse and pushed the record button.

"That's right," said Dolores. "I live on the other side of town, not too far from here. I come by—" She caught herself, pain shadowing her face. "I came by nearly every day for a chat. Gran had lots of friends, but I knew it could be lonely for her, living alone as she did. This morning, I stopped at the farmer's market first and picked out some lovely fruit and vegetables for her." Dolores dabbed at her eyes with an embroidered handkerchief. "Strawberries and wax beans and baby carrots, her favorites."

Tony prodded her gently. "So, you entered the cottage . . ."

"Gran always left the door open. It is—at least,

I used to think it was—a safe, friendly neighborhood," continued Dolores. "This morning, Gran wasn't in the kitchen or the yard, so I called upstairs for her. I thought it strange she didn't answer, so I went up to see. I've always fretted that she might fall and break a hip or some such thing, and she'd have no way of getting help." Dolores buried her face in her hands. "I never imagined, in my darkest dreams . . ."

"She was in her bedroom?" Tony asked.

Dolores struggled to recover her composure. Elizabeth's heart went out to her. "In the sitting room adjoining her bedroom," Dolores replied at last. "On the floor. She was dressed, wearing a skirt and sweater, stockings and shoes. The police said she'd been dead for— He—he must have come last evening, before she got ready for bed."

Tony glanced sharply at Elizabeth. She nodded to indicate that she'd noted Dolores's use of the pronoun "he."

"Poor Gran." Dolores shook her head. "She never had a chance against someone so brutal, so strong. . . ."

"And the fatal wound . . . was to the throat," Tony ventured.

"If she hadn't been inside her own home, I would have thought an animal had attacked her," said Dolores. "She was so ravaged . . . so bloody."

Elizabeth swallowed, fighting a wave of dizzying nausea. Tony made a note in his book. "Do you know if your grandmother had any guests last night—anyone over for supper, for example?" he asked. "Was anyone staying with her?"

"Not last night, but . . ." Dolores stopped, visibly wrestling with violent emotions. Sorrow? Elizabeth wondered. Anger? Fear?

"But what?" prompted Tony, sitting forward, his expression intense.

"Last week for a night or two . . . Robert Pembroke was here."

Elizabeth gasped. "I was right!" she burst out.

Dolores glanced at Elizabeth, startled. "He was here, Granny's old charge. She gave the best years of her life to that family, and Robert came to her in his hour of need. He came to her, and of course she took him in. All my life, I heard nothing but wonderful things about young Rob Pembroke. Gran just doted on him."

"He only stayed with her for a night or two?" asked Tony.

"He left Friday when the newspapers came out with the werewolf murders, and about how he was wanted. Gran told him she didn't believe any of it. It didn't matter to her if there was a big manhunt for him, he could stay as long as he needed to. But he said he didn't want to involve her, his own dear Nanny Millie. That's what she told me happened, and she swore me to secrecy." Dolores's eyes flashed with anger through their tears. "But there's no reason to keep the secret now, is there? Young Lord Pembroke isn't worth protecting. He's a criminal, a monster. He left, but then he came back last night—I'd bet my life on it. He came back and killed my grandmother!"

"Don't have enough cash on me for another cab ride—we'll have to take the bus," Tony told Elizabeth as they trudged down Bishop Street after concluding their interview with Dolores Price. "The bobby said there's a stop about half a mile this way. Are you up for a walk?"

"I don't mind it at all," said Elizabeth. "I need the fresh air. That was horrible in there."

"It really was," Tony agreed. "That poor, trusting old woman. What a gruesome end to a peaceful, blameless life! I feel a bit disgusted with myself, rushing out like this to record every last detail. What she was wearing when she died, her favorite fruits and vegetables, for God's sake. We're a flock of vultures, we reporters."

"You're just doing your job," Elizabeth assured him. "You were very kind to Dolores. And you heard her—she wants the story told. She wants her grandmother's murderer caught."

Tony pushed his hands deep in his trouser pockets and whistled thoughtfully through his teeth. "Why did he do it, though?" he wondered aloud. "How could he do it?"

Elizabeth shook her head. She recalled Dolores's words. *He's a criminal, a monster. . . .* "I really don't know."

Just ahead, they caught sight of the wooden bus kiosk. A bus had just pulled away from the curb. A solitary person walked away from them down the sidewalk. As they drew somewhat closer, Elizabeth's eyes widened in surprise. "Rene!" she called. "Rene, is that you?"

The young man in the dark suit turned, startled. "Why, Elizabeth," Rene said, his cheeks flushing slightly. "Fancy running into you out here!"

"Tony and I were investigating a story. What brings you to Pelham in the middle of a workday?"

"Oh, I, well—I rode the bus out to pay a call on a friend of my mother's," Rene explained. He waved vaguely over his shoulder. "She lives . . . that way."

"I thought you were always so busy at the embassy." Elizabeth smiled. "I can't believe they let you get away."

"Yes, well, a fellow deserves a lunch break every now and then," said Rene, his own smile somewhat stiff. "I'll see you at the dorm later."

Nodding good-bye, Rene hurried off. Elizabeth and Tony stepped under the bus shelter. "Just now— Did my friend seem . . . odd to you?" Elizabeth asked Tony.

"Odd? That a chap would spend his lunch hour visiting a friend of his mum's?" Tony shrugged. "Not particularly, no."

Elizabeth dismissed Rene from her thoughts. The conversation she and Tony had been engaged in was infinitely more pressing. Elizabeth tossed

Tony's question back at him. "Why do you think he did it? Why kill Mildred Price?"

Tony jingled the loose change in his pocket. "Because the werewolf . . . Robert Pembroke . . . is more desperate than ever," he theorized grimly. "He must have confided in Nanny Millie, or perhaps he only suspected that she'd guessed the truth about him. Then, fearing that she'd turn him in to the authorities, he silenced her."

It was coldly, perfectly logical. Elizabeth shuddered. "He has no mercy."

"None." Tony fixed a somber gaze on Elizabeth. "And that's why you mustn't pull any more stunts like yesterday's break-in at Neville's," he ordered. "I know you're hot to break open this case, and I am, too, but I can't let you investigate on your own. It's far too dangerous. Promise me, Elizabeth. If you must go out on a limb, take someone with you—me, or your young man Luke, or Jessica."

"I promise," Elizabeth said reluctantly. "I'll be careful. But I'm not likely to enlist Jessica's help. She still won't acknowledge that Robert's guilty— even this won't convince her, I bet." Elizabeth grew riled just thinking about it. "For some insane reason, she's blaming everything bad that's happened on me. In case you haven't picked up on it, we're not speaking to each other."

"This is no time for petty sibling quarrels," Tony responded with uncharacteristic sternness. He gripped Elizabeth's arm and she blinked up at him, startled. "You need each other more than ever, can't you see that?" His eyes burned into hers and she felt a thrill of excitement, and fear. "This . . . thing . . . is incredibly powerful, and incredibly evil. Our only hope of defeating it lies in banding together. Only that way, can we counter his strength, foil him in his wicked designs. Don't let yourself become the weak link, Elizabeth. Don't place yourself in the wolfman's path."

The door to the bedroom swung open and the intruder padded in on silent feet. Rearing back his head, his nostrils flared and he inhaled the feminine scents of the three girls who lived there—the perfumes, the shampoos and lotions, the delicate fabrics of their clothing.

One of the three girls held no interest for him, but the other two . . .

They have something of mine. They have something that can hurt me. That's why they went to Dr. Neville's.

Nanny Millie was out of the way, but the Wakefield twins still posed a threat, he knew it. He prowled over to a dressing table, his bloodshot eyes darting around the room. Yanking open a drawer, he pawed through the clothing, searching. Finding nothing, he hurled the stockings and slips and nightgowns angrily on the floor.

The next drawer yielded books and letters, one with the name Todd Wilkins on the return address.

He snarled, ripping the letter in two with his teeth. Then, glimpsing the manila folder at the bottom of the drawer, his eyes brightened. He removed it, reading the label: Robert Pembroke, Jr. *This is good, but it isn't all.*

He searched drawer after drawer, finding nothing. Panting and desperate, he ripped the sheets from the beds, slashed the pillows with his fingernails until feathers flew through the air like a snowstorm.

Under the mattress of one of the top bunks, he made his second discovery. Another one of Dr. Neville's files! With a triumphant yowl, he seized it. Annabelle S. *So they had found her, found out about her . . .*

Clever, clever, clever, hiding it so carefully, he thought as he paced the room. What else was hidden there? There was something—something important, essential, fateful. Yes—the silver bullet! *I must find it.*

He clawed through the dresser drawers again. Tearing the closet door half off its hinges, he dug through piles of shoes, tossed armfuls of jackets and dresses onto the floor.

Frustration boiled up inside him like volcanic lava. He ripped the room to pieces looking for the bullet, but to no avail. *They still have it,* he thought, slinking out of the room, out of the dorm, into the sheltering shadows of the park. *They are my enemies, then, to the death.*

Chapter 6

"This is shaping up nicely," Lucy said to Jessica late Monday afternoon after skimming Jessica's preliminary draft of a short biographical piece that would accompany Lucy's airline merger feature. "Sharp, stylish, succinct. You know, you could be a fine writer someday."

Jessica lifted her shoulders in a careless shrug. Her twin sister would do cartwheels over such praise from the editor-in-chief of the *London Journal*, but being a writer wasn't exactly Jessica's life's ambition. "Thanks."

"I'll scribble some comments and you can take a final crack at it in the morning. I guess that's all for today. You've been a terrific help."

"It was fun," Jessica said sincerely. "I'm really psyched to be your intern. See you tomorrow."

Her new desk was in the main newsroom just a

few steps from Lucy's office. *Miles away from Elizabeth and Tony,* Jessica thought as she sat down and reached under the desk for her shoulder bag. *But it's still not far enough.*

The whole office had been buzzing all afternoon, ever since Tony and Elizabeth returned from Pelham with a melodramatic accounting of the werewolf-style murder of the former Pembroke family nanny. Elizabeth hadn't spoken to Jessica about it, but a couple of times when they'd been in the same general vicinity, Jessica had caught her sister directing superior, self-righteous glances her way.

She's so sure she has it all figured out, Jessica fumed, unzipping the inside pocket of her bag and feeling around for a lipstick. *She acts like she's the head of Scotland Yard or something.* Instead of a lipstick case, her hand touched something cool and hard and unfamiliar. *A coin?* Jessica thought. *No, there's a chain attached. Jewelry . . . but what . . . ?*

Pulling a tarnished silver pendant from her purse, she recognized it immediately. "It's the tacky voodoo charm Luke gave Liz," Jessica muttered, tossing it disdainfully on her desk. "I can't believe she put it in there." Her anger flared. "She thinks Robert is the werewolf and is going to come after me!"

If it weren't so nasty, it would almost be funny, she reflected bitterly. *Sensible, smarty-pants Elizabeth, of all people, turning out to be totally, idiotically superstitious.*

Jessica glared at the pendant—at the face of the wolf baring its fangs inside the five-pointed star. An unaccountable shiver chased up her spine. Maybe there was some magic at work there. . . .

"No, it's just a stupid toy," she told herself. But against her will, she found herself picking up the pendant and looking at it more closely. The silver was solid, heavy—reassuring somehow. It quickly grew warm in her hand. Her first instinct had been to stalk over to Elizabeth's desk and throw the necklace in her face, but now Jessica didn't want to let it go.

She must have hated to part with it, Jessica mused. *Such a special gift from lover-boy. I guess she really is worried about me.*

The faintest, most begrudging of smiles curved Jessica's lips. Even though she was furious at her sister, she couldn't help being a tiny bit touched by Elizabeth's concern. *We haven't talked in days, but she's thinking about me,* Jessica realized. *She's worrying about me. Even though, of course, she's totally barking up the wrong tree—Robert hasn't committed any crimes and he wouldn't hurt me in a million years.*

Thoughtfully, Jessica turned the pendant over in her hand. On the back, a single initial had been engraved: a fancy, script "A," now nearly worn off. Jessica traced the letter with her fingertip. Something about it triggered a fuzzy, indefinite memory . . . but of what? She shook her head with a sigh. *It doesn't mean anything. It's just a letter, just someone's initial, the person who originally owned the necklace.*

She looked again at the werewolf and pentagram. "I'm not in any danger," she murmured to herself, "so I don't need any hoodoo voodoo potions and charms to protect me. But . . ." But she couldn't deny it. She wanted to clasp the smooth silver chain around her throat, to feel the pendant resting warm and heavy against her skin. "It is kind of pretty, kind of interesting."

Reaching back underneath her hair, Jessica fastened the necklace. *I'll wear it, but not so anyone can see,* she decided, tucking the pendant into her shirt. *There's no way I'm going to give Liz the satisfaction . . . !*

At the end of the day, Tony slipped his arms in the sleeves of his tweed jacket. Gripping the handle of his briefcase, he headed for the street.

Halfway across the newsroom, he halted. The editor-in-chief's door was ajar, and he could see Lucy still reading through some copy, her pumps kicked off and her stockinged feet on top of her desk.

Loosening his tie, Tony stuck his head in her office, smiling. "Good night, boss."

She didn't look up from her papers. "Night, Frank."

Tony lingered. "Uh, by the way. What did you think of my Mildred Price murder piece?"

Lucy glanced at him over the rims of her glasses. "Top-notch. I was impressed."

Tony practically levitated with joy at the compliment. Before he realized what he was saying, the words he'd been dying to utter for weeks spilled from his lips. "So, what do you say we talk about crime over a pint of ale and a bite of supper?"

Instantly, Tony regretted his audacity. "I'm not ready to call it a day yet," Lucy replied, her tone cool. "And besides. I have a philosophy, which I shared this morning with Jessica, about keeping one's private life out of the workplace. Let's keep it straight: you and I have a professional relationship, Frank. At least, that's what I'd call it on a good day," she added dryly.

"Point taken," Tony said with forced carelessness. "We all need to eat, that's all I was getting at. See you tomorrow."

He walked away whistling—he wouldn't give Lucy the satisfaction of seeing that she'd burst his dearest hopes like a balloon. But as soon as he was out of sight of her office, Tony's shoulders slumped dejectedly. *I guess that's it, ol' chap,* he thought to himself with a sigh. *It's hopeless.*

It was a gray London twilight as the twins walked in silence to the tube station a few blocks from the *London Journal* offices. Without exchanging a single word, they'd managed to leave the office at the same time, thanks to Jessica sauntering slowly by Elizabeth's desk and then waiting by the door, tapping her foot, until Elizabeth joined her.

She may be too blind to see that Robert is the werewolf, but she's not a complete idiot, Elizabeth reflected as they waited on the underground platform for the train. *She knows it's safer to stick together like this than to strike out on our own, especially after dark. She hasn't forgotten what happened to her down here last week. . . .*

Far away, they heard a rumbling. It grew louder and closer. Bright lights and a high-pitched metallic screeching filled the tunnel and a train roared into view. Car after car after car swept past as the train came to a stop.

There were quite a few other commuters standing on the platform, all dressed in work clothes and appearing sane and normal and nonthreatening; still, Elizabeth heaved a secret sigh of relief as she and Jessica sat down in a crowded car and the train leapt forward to speed like a bullet through the tunnel. *Why does life in London lately feel like one close call after another?* she wondered wearily. *Some vacation this is turning out to be!*

After a minute, the train rocked to a stop. People stood up and got off; others boarded and took the vacated seats. As the train proceeded, Elizabeth opened her mouth to ask Jessica a question. She was curious, and a little jealous: how had Jessica managed to get herself appointed Lucy's personal intern? What was it like working for the editor-in-chief?

But I'm not talking to her, Elizabeth reminded herself. *I'll have to ask Luke or Tony for the dirt.*

Jessica, meanwhile, glanced at Elizabeth out of the corner of her eye. Then, staring straight ahead, she said, as if to herself, "For such a smart, successful woman, Lucy Friday can really be a dope. Tony is so cute—all the women in the office think so. And she could have him, just like that." Jessica snapped her fingers to illustrate the point. "Why doesn't she snag him while she has the chance?"

"She's crazy about him and he's crazy about her, but they won't admit it," Elizabeth reflected, looking around idly—at everything and everyone but Jessica. "Tony thinks someone as feisty and brilliant as Lucy could never consider an ordinary chap like him, and Lucy thinks she's above romance—she thinks falling in love is incompatible with being a top-notch journalist."

"Now that she's the big boss and he's one of her underlings, they'll never get it together," Jessica concluded.

"Not without some help, anyway," mumbled Elizabeth. "Like a major push from a third party."

She felt a nostalgic pang and wondered if Jessica was thinking the same thing she was. *This would have been a natural for us in the old days. If we teamed up, it would take about five seconds to hatch up a plot to throw Lucy and Tony into each other's arms.* But if Jessica was entertaining fond reminiscences of past sisterly conspiracies, she didn't show it. Chin in the air, she kept a cool and expressionless profile turned to Elizabeth. Silence encircled them again, and this time it seemed unbreakable.

The underground ride, and their walk from the station to HIS, was uneventful. Entering the dorm, Jessica and Elizabeth climbed the stairs to the third floor, still in silence. When they opened their bedroom door, however, they both cried out simultaneously. "Ohmigod, what happened?" Jessica screeched.

"We've been robbed—ransacked," Elizabeth gasped.

Together, they stared at the wreckage of their room. Dresser drawers had been emptied willy-nilly on the floor, sheets and pillows thrown off the beds, the closets tumbled. Jessica put a hand over her mouth, speechless. Elizabeth also stood like a statue, paralyzed with shock.

Just then, they heard a sharp intake of breath behind them. Elizabeth jumped, her heart in her throat.

It was only Portia, who'd just returned from a rehearsal at the theater; there were no play performances on Monday evenings. "There's been an intruder," Portia exclaimed, her gray eyes wide. "Oh, look at that mess! I'll run down to Mrs. Bates and we'll call the police. You two start going through your things to find out what's missing."

94

Portia dashed off down the hall. Elizabeth took a tentative step into the room, her skin crawling. *An intruder . . . what if he's still here?* Her eyes darted to the open closet, its contents spilling out into the room. No, there was no place to hide—everything was torn open, exposed.

Jessica crossed the room, stirring up a cloud of goose feathers from the shredded pillows, and began sifting through her scattered belongings. "My jewelry's still here, and my money," she announced, holding up a quilted pouch.

"Mine, too," said Elizabeth. Bending, she picked up a torn fragment of notepaper. "My letter from Todd, all torn up! Who . . . why?"

"Look, Portia's dresser was hardly touched," Jessica observed.

Elizabeth glanced over. "Her bed, either."

"If the person didn't want to take money and jewelry, what did they want?" Jessica wondered. "Why do . . . this?"

"He—or she—must have been looking for something," Elizabeth said. She turned back to her dresser. "But what? And did he find it?"

Elizabeth kicked at a pile of things on the floor, then checked her drawers again. *Wait a minute,* she thought. Something was missing—the file she'd taken from Dr. Neville's!

"My file!" Elizabeth said out loud even as she realized that something else even more important had disappeared.

"My file!" Jessica burst out at the exact same moment.

The two sisters stared at each other. "And the silver bullet Luke gave me," Elizabeth gasped. "It's gone!"

"Silver bullet, I say, just like the movies, what?"

Both girls whirled. Sergeant Bumpo of Scotland Yard stood in the doorway, scratching his bald head.

"Oh, no," Jessica muttered, exchanging a glance with her sister. "I can't believe they sent him!"

If she weren't so upset, she would have laughed. Their very first day at the *London Journal*, Lucy Friday, then the crime editor, had assigned the twins to Sergeant Bumpo's beat. Initially, they'd been psyched as they fantasized about helping Scotland Yard crack open its toughest cases. It didn't take long to figure out, however, that Sergeant Bumpo was a comically inept buffoon who couldn't catch a criminal if his life depended on it.

They only give him the stupid, trivial cases, Jessica thought as the portly, red-faced detective stumbled into the room, tripping over a pile of clothes the intruder had dumped from a drawer. When Mrs. Bates called, the police must have written it off as a dorm prank.

"Yes, a silver bullet," Elizabeth explained. "It . . . it was just a trinket, a charm for a charm bracelet."

"Any other jewelry stolen?" asked Bumpo, wandering aimlessly around the disheveled room, pausing occasionally to examine something with a wise nod, as if he'd found a significant clue. *You can't fool me, Bumpo,* Jessica thought scornfully. *You're just going through the motions—you don't have the faintest idea what to look for!*

"No, no valuables—no money," said Elizabeth. "Only a file folder. Something I brought home from work, something worthless."

Elizabeth glanced at Jessica. Jessica cleared her throat. "Yes, a file of mine is missing, too." Not wanting to say anything about searching Dr. Neville's apartment, she simply repeated Elizabeth's remarks. "Something from work—I can't imagine why anyone would have thought it was interesting."

"Perhaps it was just a few of the boys from the dormitory having a lark, eh?" Bumpo proposed, appearing relieved that the case might wrap up so quickly and harmlessly.

"A lark?" Elizabeth glared at him. "Hardly! Whoever did this was violent—vicious."

"Well, hmm, I don't see why—if nothing was— but perhaps—" Sergeant Bumpo blustered.

Portia and Mrs. Bates had appeared in the doorway. Now Portia stepped into the room. "If it wasn't just an ordinary, random robber, can you think of anyone who might have wanted something from you?" Portia asked Jessica and Elizabeth. "To hurt you, or to take something from you?"

"Yes, of course, that was going to be my next

question. Right-o," interjected Bumpo, puffing out his chest and looking important. "Can you provide us with a list of possible suspects?"

Jessica felt Elizabeth's eyes boring into her. A nervous flush stole up her neck, staining her whole face pink. *Robert was here this morning, I know it*, Jessica thought, remembering her powerful intuition. *What if he had come back later and . . . ?*

"I have no idea who it might have been," Jessica told Sergeant Bumpo, her voice coming out in a nervous squeak.

Elizabeth continued to stare at Jessica hard. Jessica didn't meet her sister's gaze. Finally, Elizabeth shook her head. "Me, either," she said quietly.

"Well, I'll make a full report," Bumpo promised, giving the girls a gallant salute and marching toward the door. The closet door.

"What have we . . . ? Hmm, I say—" Bumpo backed up. More red-faced than ever, he took another shot at an exit, this time fortuitously landing in the hallway where a distracted Mrs. Bates stood wringing her hands. "Ring us up if you find anything else missing," the detective instructed the girls. "Cheerio!"

Elizabeth, Jessica, and Portia waved good-bye and Mrs. Bates accompanied Sergeant Bumpo down the hall. A moment later, there was a crashing sound, as if someone had fallen down the stairs. "My heavens," Portia declared, laughing. "I can't say that pathetic performance gives me much faith in Sergeant Bumpo's powers of detection, unless, of course, he's some kind of idiot savant."

"No, he's just an idiot, period," complained Elizabeth. "Talk about incompetence. He didn't come up with a single clue—he didn't even dust for fingerprints. We'll never know who did this!"

Jessica kept quiet. She was starting to feel glad that Bumpo had been sent to investigate, rather than someone else who might actually have found something. *I mean, of course it would be great if they catch the person, as it wasn't Robert,* she thought. *But just in case . . .*

Portia and Elizabeth began to clean up the room. Depressed and still more than a bit shaken, Jessica collapsed in an easy chair by the window. "Just leave my things," she told the other two. "I'll pick them up later."

Portia crossed the room to put a hand on Jessica's shoulder, giving her a warm, supportive squeeze. "Don't fret, Jess. Mrs. Bates will keep us all safe and sound. She's already sent David off to have copies of her front-door key made so we can each carry one—starting tonight, the dorm will be locked day and night. Besides," she joked, pointing out the window. "It looks like Bumpo's already got your man!"

Jessica peered into the gloomy dusk. Under a streetlight below, she saw a homeless man in a brown coat and cap weaving and shouting.

Elizabeth stepped over to the window to look. "I saw that man in the park the other day. He seemed harmless, but I guess he's drunk and causing a nuisance."

"I've seen him before, too," Jessica said, stifling a melancholy sigh. *This morning, when I ran outside looking for Robert.*

All three watched as the hapless detective struggled to get a pair of handcuffs on the uncooperative vagrant. "Poor Bumpo," they said in unison.

"Come on, Jessica," Portia urged a short while later, grabbing Jessica's hand and dragging her to her feet. "Let's go to supper—some hot soup will buck you up. Join us, Liz?"

"I'm going out in a bit, actually," Elizabeth replied. "See you later."

The door had only just closed behind Portia and Jessica when someone rapped sharply on it. "Come in," Elizabeth called.

Rene burst into the room. "Elizabeth!" he cried, dashing forward to take both her hands in his. "I just returned from the embassy and heard about the vandalism from Mrs. Bates. Are you all right?"

Rene squeezed her hands tightly and Elizabeth returned the pressure, smiling to reassure him. "I'm fine. It was pretty much of a mess, though."

"Thank goodness it was just the room that got torn apart." Rene's expression grew even more anxious and dark. "What if you or Jessica had been here when the perpetrator came in? What if—"

"Well, we weren't," Elizabeth cut in. "We're fine, really. Don't worry about us."

"I am worried," said Rene, "and you should be, too. I'm sure this wasn't a random act, Elizabeth. Someone is after you. You and Jessica must leave London immediately."

The urgency of Rene's tone struck an emotional chord in Elizabeth. She was more frightened than ever at the thought that the killer had penetrated the sanctuary of HIS, but she wasn't going to admit it. "Didn't we already have this conversation, Rene? We can't leave London," she reasoned. "It doesn't make sense, and besides it's not necessary. The police are investigating and they'll probably catch the person who did it and it will probably turn out to have nothing to do with the murders."

"You don't know that," insisted Rene. "And Portia told me about the detective who was here— a real clown, apparently. Please, Elizabeth. You and Jessica could spend the night at the embassy or a hotel and be on a plane home to the U.S. first thing in the morning. I'll make all the arrangements."

"No." Elizabeth shook her head firmly. "I appreciate your concern, Rene, but I'm staying in London and that's that. And now, I'm on my way out. Luke and I have a movie date."

Rene frowned. "Stay inside, Elizabeth," he begged. "Don't go out into the night."

Slipping on a jacket, Elizabeth laughed. "I'll be OK," she assured Rene. "Come on, walk downstairs with me."

Rene walked her to the front door of the dorm. As Elizabeth eased it open, she did have a brief instant of apprehension. *What if someone is out there, watching, waiting for another opportunity to strike?* she thought with a shiver.

But as she saw Luke striding up the walk, a welcoming smile on his face, her fears vanished like mist in the sun. The dark night held no danger, as long as Luke was by her side. "I'll be with Luke," Elizabeth told Rene as she stepped out the door and waved good-bye. "I'll be perfectly safe."

The top bunk creaked as Jessica rolled over. She burrowed more deeply under the covers, just the tip of her nose and her eyes peeking out.

The room is so dark, she thought, clenching her teeth to keep them from chattering. She felt like a baby, but she wished there were a night-light— something—*anything, but this spooky, haunted blackness.*

There's barely even a moon, Jessica noted, gazing out at the thin cold crescent visible through a break in the clouds. She remembered the full moon shining over Pembroke Manor the night Joy Singleton was murdered. *Maybe darkness isn't the worst thing,* Jessica decided with a shudder. *It's better than a full moon drawing the werewolf out of his lair!*

102

When she and Elizabeth had first arrived in London, they'd joked about the movie *An American Werewolf in London*, which they saw at a going-away party Lila Fowler gave for them before they went abroad. When Elizabeth and Luke started taking the werewolf business seriously, Jessica had ridiculed them. She was still highly skeptical that the murderer was actually a werewolf, but there was no doubt that the person responsible for the bloody rampage was less than human.

And there was also no doubt that Jessica Wakefield was scared out of her wits.

It's getting closer, she thought, wishing she could will the hands of the clock to speed forward toward sunrise. *The evil. It was here.*

She couldn't stop thinking about the smell of Robert's cologne lingering in her room. Once more, she forced herself to consider head-on the possibility that Robert had been the intruder. *No,* she concluded at last, her spirits lifting somewhat. *No. I know him. Yes, he's on the run—he's hiding somewhere, he's hiding something—but he didn't ransack this place. It just doesn't make sense. He wouldn't have made my bed for me in the morning and then come back later to tear it apart.*

Then who did? There were so many baffling questions. *Why was Robert here this morning?* Jessica asked herself, hugging her pillow. *Why didn't he leave a note—why doesn't he call me at work?*

And why did the intruder, whoever it was, steal the Annabelle S. file and Liz's stupid silver bullet?

Annabelle S., Annabelle S., she mused, her hand straying to her throat and the silver pendant. Suddenly, it hit her. The "A" on the pendant. What if it stood for Annabelle?

"Elizabeth!" Jessica hissed. "Elizabeth, wake up!"

"Hmm?" Elizabeth mumbled sleepily.

Jessica hung over the side of the bed. "I found the werewolf necklace you put in my purse," she whispered down to her sister. "It's Luke's, right? Where did he get it?"

"I thought we weren't talking," Elizabeth said, sounding tired and crabby.

"We're not. Just tell me where he got it."

Elizabeth rubbed her eyes. "His mother gave it to him."

His mother! Jessica's heart raced. Luke's mother was dead and so was Annabelle S. Annabelle S. could be Luke's mother—the S. could stand for Shepherd! "What was her name?" Jessica asked excitedly.

"Ann. Why?"

Ann, not Annabelle. *So much for that brilliant idea,* Jessica thought, disappointed. "No reason. Go back to sleep."

Jessica punched her pillow, frustrated and mystified. *Who on earth was Annabelle S.?* she wondered for about the thousandth time. She still didn't know, but Jessica felt certain now that

Annabelle S., dead for nine years, mattered some-how. Somehow, she figured into the puzzle. *Because the person who trashed our room took the file,* thought Jessica. *Maybe that's why he broke in in the first place!* Although that didn't really make sense, because who but the ghost of Dr. Neville could have known she had the file?

Jessica's eyelids drooped sleepily. The mystery had more angles every day, and it tired her out just thinking about it. She'd just have to redouble her investigative efforts in the morning.

Elizabeth lay in the dark, listening to her sister's steady breathing. Jessica had obviously dozed off, but now, Elizabeth was wide awake . . . and spooked.

Her skin crawled, thinking about a stranger entering their room, opening their drawers and closet, tearing the sheets off the beds. *Touching my clothes,* Elizabeth thought. *Reading my letters . . .*

She hadn't said anything to Sergeant Bumpo about Robert Pembroke. On the surface, there was no reason to connect the ransacked room with the manhunt for the alleged murderer, and Jessica's eyes had seemed to plead with her not to mention Robert's name. *But who else would want that medical file?* Elizabeth wondered. *And the silver bullet? It must have been the werewolf . . . Robert Pembroke himself.*

105

Elizabeth squeezed her eyes shut, trying to get back into the mood she'd been in on her date with Luke. After grabbing a bite to eat, they'd seen a movie, a lighthearted romantic comedy. Instead of the comedy, though, Elizabeth found herself thinking about another film she and Luke had gone to recently—*The Howling*, a horror movie. A werewolf movie . . .

Elizabeth heard a faint creaking sound and she held her breath, her heart thumping. What if the person who trashed the room came back?

The sound wasn't repeated; it was just the old house settling, Elizabeth decided. But she couldn't quite shake the sensation that something was stirring in the night, a shadowy, palpable presence. A werewolf's victims can't rest until their killer is destroyed, Elizabeth recalled, thinking about the storyline of *An American Werewolf in London*. Maybe all those poor lost souls are walking the earth: Nurse Handley, Dr. Neville, Joy, Maria the cook, Mrs. Price . . .

Gradually, Elizabeth slipped back into a troubled sleep, only to be visited again by the nightmare she'd had as the full moon hung over Pembroke Manor, the night Joy Singleton was murdered in Jessica's bed. Elizabeth stood helpless as the werewolf chased her sister, as he grasped Jessica with hairy, muscular arms, as he bent with a howl to tear her throat with his teeth. . . .

Wait a minute. . . . In her dream, Elizabeth

heard the snarl close to her own ear; she felt the claws digging into her flesh, the hot breath against her throat, the point of a knife-sharp fang. This time, the girl the werewolf was pursuing was herself.

Chapter 7

Jessica was just finishing her breakfast on Tuesday morning when her sister hurried into the dining room. She glanced at the clock over the mantel with a feeling of satisfaction. *Aha—look who overslept!* Jessica gloated silently. *Someone's going to be late for work today, and it's not me. For once, Liz will have to scramble—serves her right.*

As she walked to the tube station, however, Jessica's hard heart softened somewhat. She thought about the scene in the dorm room the previous evening, when they'd arrived home to find the place ransacked. *Sergeant Bumpo asked if we had any suspicions about who might have done it, and Liz looked right at me and I know she was thinking about Robert. But for once, she kept her big mouth shut.*

I should probably be grateful for small favors,

Jessica decided grudgingly. Stopping at a news-stand near the entrance to the tube, she lingered for ten minutes glancing through various glossy European fashion magazines. Just as she was about to blow Elizabeth off, her sister trotted up, pant-ing. Without exchanging a word, the twins de-scended the escalator together.

A quarter of an hour later, as they pushed through the revolving doors of the newspaper building, Jessica experienced a strange feeling of déjà vu. An atmosphere of tense excitement filled the office; people were dashing distractedly in all directions. "This reminds me of the first day we came here," Jessica said, then bit her lip as she re-alized she'd inadvertently spoken to her sister. *A big story must be breaking,* she added to herself. *A story as big as the Dr. Neville murder!*

Immediately, a feeling of foreboding washed over her. "Please, God, not another murder," she heard Elizabeth whisper.

They hurried forward and Jessica grabbed a pass-ing colleague by the arm. "Zena, what's going on?"

"There's been another attack—the werewolf struck again," Zena said dramatically. "The owner of the *Journal*, Lord Pembroke, was the victim!"

"Lord Pembroke!" Jessica gasped. Her knees buckled and a misty gray curtain seemed to fall be-fore her eyes; she staggered forward, on the verge of fainting. "Ohmigod, Robert's father."

Elizabeth grabbed Jessica's elbow to support

her. "Lord Pembroke, dead!" she exclaimed. "I can't believe it."

"No, no, he's not dead," said Zena. "Not yet, anyway. He's in hospital. He survived the attack."

At Zena's words, Jessica snapped back into focus. Still pale, she shook off Elizabeth's arm and gaped at Zena. "He survived? Did he . . . did he get a look at— Did he identify his attacker?"

Please, don't let it be Robert, Jessica chanted in her brain. *Please, don't let it, don't let it, don't let it . . .*

Zena shook her head. "Supposedly, he didn't get a good look at the fellow. Or should I say creature? We don't have much information—the police weren't able to interview Lord Pembroke at any length. He's in critical condition."

"But there's no doubt it was the same person who killed the others?" said Elizabeth. "He was wounded in the same way?"

Zena nodded. "The throat," she said simply.

While Elizabeth plied Zena with more questions, Jessica wandered over to her desk near the editor-in-chief's office, dazed. *Lord Pembroke, brutally attacked!* she thought. *The poor, poor man.* Robert's father had been kind to Jessica, and she had a soft spot for him. *Critical condition— that's pretty bad. What if he doesn't make it? What will Robert do?*

A sudden, devastating thought struck Jessica. Robert had disappeared—he could be far away, completely out of touch with the world. *What if he hasn't heard about this? What if Lord Pembroke dies in the hospital, and Robert isn't there to hold his hand, to say good-bye?*

"Jessica. Hullo, Jessica!"

Jessica blinked. Lucy Friday was standing in front of her desk, briskly snapping her fingers. "Oh, I'm sorry," said Jessica, her face flooding with color. "Do you have work for me? I was just—we heard when we came in— Oh, I'm so worried, about Lord Pembroke Senior and Robert and everything!"

She sniffled and gulped, on the verge of bursting into tears. In typical no-nonsense fashion, Lucy thrust a handkerchief at her. "Blow your nose and get yourself together," Lucy recommended, not unkindly. "Then come to my office."

Dutifully, Jessica blew her nose. Running over to the ladies' room, she splashed water on her face and brushed her hair. As she took a few deep breaths, gradually some of the tension began to drain from her body.

Her eyes dry, Jessica presented herself at Lucy's desk. Lucy waved her into a chair. "Now, are you just distressed in general or is there something specific troubling you?" she asked.

"I have to find Robert," said Jessica, anxiously clasping her hands together. "He's hiding somewhere—he might not even know about all this. I have to tell him."

112

"Hmm." Lucy tapped a pen on the desk. "What would you think if I told you it's more probable that Robert does know," she said flatly, "because he himself is the attacker?"

Jessica's eyes flashed. She responded without thinking. "I'd think maybe you weren't the great journalist you're cracked up to be. I'd think you were just listening to the stories everybody else was telling without going out there and finding out the truth for yourself."

Lucy stared at Jessica, momentarily taken aback. Then she smiled broadly. "You've got guts, Wakefield," she declared. "I admire that in a person. And even though I believe, for very good reasons and not just on the basis of hearsay, that Robert Pembroke Junior is guilty as all get-out, I sympathize with your situation. Take the morning off. Get to the bottom of this. Find Robert, if you can."

"But how?" Jessica asked.

Lucy considered for a moment. "Why don't you talk to Lord Pembroke?" she suggested at last. "He may know more about his son's whereabouts than he's let on to the police—he may still be protecting Robert."

Elizabeth, Luke, and Tony sat in chairs clustered around Tony's desk, cups of steaming tea in their hands. "Lord Pembroke was attacked in his study at Pembroke Green, the family's London residence," Tony related. Elizabeth thought he sounded congested, as if he were coming down with a cold. "Around midnight, as he enjoyed a quiet, solitary pipe by candlelight before retiring."

Elizabeth shivered. "How could Rob—could anyone do such a thing?" she asked. "His own . . ."

She couldn't bear to put it into words. Luke, however, had no such hesitations. "His own father," he exclaimed, his eyes glittering strangely. "To try to kill one's own father!"

"It's the most heinous crime he's attempted yet," Tony agreed. "Clearly the boy went after his father to get back at him for turning against him."

"And also to prevent Lord Pembroke Senior from turning him in to the authorities," contributed Elizabeth.

"The werewolf's cruelty and fury knows no bounds," said Luke. "He knows no limits. Nothing . . . no one . . . is sacred."

Elizabeth and Tony both stared at Luke. Tony nodded, although Elizabeth could tell he thought Luke a bit batty. Even Elizabeth at times had to admit that Luke took things to an extreme. Poets are just like that, she'd tell herself.

But this morning, Luke's ominous, prophetic words seemed more than appropriate to the circumstances. *Maybe Robert's not a werewolf like the ones we see in the movies*, Elizabeth thought, *but he's a monster. The animal side of his nature has taken over.*

Another shiver shook her body from head to

toe. She'd decided not to tell Tony and Luke about the break-in at the dorm because she didn't want to worry them, but this latest development cast a new and terrible light on the incident. *The werewolf was in our room, and then he went to Pembroke Green. What if Jess or I had been home? Right now would one of us be lying in a hospital bed . . . or in the morgue?*

"It won't be long now, though," mused Tony, tipping back in his chair. "He's on the run, desperate, taking bigger risks than ever. And he's getting sloppy. He didn't finish the job—he left one alive."

Out of the corner of her eye, Elizabeth glimpsed a blur of color. Glancing over, she saw Jessica, in a bright yellow skirt and jacket and with her bag slung over her shoulder, dashing out the door of the office.

Elizabeth bit her lip anxiously. Where was Jessica off to in such a hurry? Was she planning to take bigger risks than ever, in the name of a misguided love? Could she still believe in Robert's innocence after this?

At enormous, sprawling London Hospital, Jessica learned from the receptionist that Lord Pembroke had been moved from intensive care to a private room on the third floor of Wing C.

"You're not from one of the newspapers, are you?" the receptionist asked suspiciously. "We'll have no reporters up there. A security guard just

115

hauled off that sneaky young man from the *London Daily Post*."

"Oh, no, I'm just a friend of the family," said Jessica.

She had to give the nurse on duty the same assurances. "All right," the nurse agreed, after eyeing Jessica up and down. "You can go in. But his wife is with him at the moment."

"I'll wait, then," Jessica murmured. "I don't want to disturb them."

A few minutes later, from her seat in the corner of the visitors' lounge, Jessica saw Lady Pembroke emerge from Room 21. The older woman was dabbing her eyes with a handkerchief; her thin face, always perfectly made-up, looked crumpled and careworn. Jessica had gotten the impression that the Pembroke marriage was mostly one of appearances at this point, but there must have been a trace of love left somewhere. Lady Pembroke was so distracted and upset, she didn't even notice Jessica as she walked past the lounge on her way to the nurses' station.

Rising, Jessica slipped unobtrusively into Room 21. Curtains darkened the windows; except for the sound of labored breathing, the room was silent.

At the sight of Lord Pembroke, tears of pity sprang into Jessica's eyes. A thick bandage muffled his throat; there was a tube in his nose to help him breathe and an IV hooked into his arm. The once

116

hearty, vigorous man looked pale, diminished, and old, his body thin and frail under the sheet.

Lord Pembroke's eyes were closed. *Is he asleep?* Jessica wondered. *Unconscious?* She pulled a chair close to the bedside. "Lord Pembroke," she said softly. "It's Jessica Wakefield. How are you feeling?"

Lord Pembroke's eyelids fluttered, then opened. He gazed up at Jessica, but he didn't seem to really see her. "I wanted to catch a werewolf," he muttered.

He wanted to catch a werewolf? He must be hallucinating. "What do you mean?"

She had to lean close to hear his disjointed words. "My hobby . . . our hobby. I stalled the police investigation, thinking I might—but when the evidence started to point to my boy . . . Too many hurt, too many dead . . ."

Jessica patted his arm. "Ssh," she murmured. "Don't strain yourself."

Lord Pembroke made a visible effort to focus on her. A faint smile touched his haggard face. "My son loves you," he whispered.

Jessica took the thin hand that lay on top of the covers and squeezed it gently, her eyes brimming.

"He was a troublemaker as a boy, but he could never hurt anyone," Lord Pembroke continued. "Especially not his beloved nanny, or his own father . . ."

"I know," Jessica said. "I know."

Lord Pembroke continued to look up at her, his

117

gaze fond but foggy. Then suddenly, the expression in his eyes sharpened—they flashed with fire and he sat up in bed, fully awake. "The pendant," he declared accusingly. "Where did you get that?"

As she bent forward, Luke's silver werewolf pendant had slipped from behind the collar of Jessica's blouse. Startled, she raised a hand to tuck it back in. "My—my sister gave it to me," she stuttered. "It's—"

"Forgive me." Lord Pembroke's eyelids fluttered; he sank back weakly on the bed. "I didn't mean to scare you, my dear. It's just that it reminds me of the one I gave poor Annabelle."

"Annabelle?" Alarm bells sounded in Jessica's head. The file from Dr. Neville's—Annabelle S.!

"My lovely Annabelle," Lord Pembroke murmured. "The only woman I ever really . . ."

His voice trailed off; he seemed to be slipping back into semiconsciousness. Jessica gripped his hand, jiggling his arm a bit. She wasn't about to let him drift off to sleep now, not when she was on the verge of an important discovery. "Annabelle," she prompted, her tone urgent. "Who is she?"

When Lord Pembroke spoke again, it was clear his mind had gone off in another direction. "You must tell Robert something for me," he said.

Jessica sighed, swallowing her disappointment at not learning more about Annabelle. "Anything."

"Tell him . . ." Lord Pembroke's breathing was raspy and labored; every word was a struggle. "He has . . . a . . . brother."

"A brother?" Jessica gasped. "But . . ." But Robert was an only child! Or rather, she realized, Robert was the only child Lord Pembroke Senior had with Lady Pembroke. . . .

Her head whirled. Was Lord Pembroke trying to say that he'd had another son with another woman? That Robert had an illegitimate half brother he didn't even know about?

"Tell him," Lord Pembroke repeated feebly.

"Yes, of course," Jessica promised. "If I ever see him again, that is."

"You'll see him," Lord Pembroke assured her, his eyes closing. His final words were uttered in the faintest of whispers, but Jessica heard them and held them close to her heart. "He'll come back to you. He loves you. . . ."

Hunched over her desk at the *Journal*, Elizabeth thumbed through the notebook she'd been using to record interviews and observations relating to the werewolf case. *We know so much, and yet so little,* she thought, chewing on the end of a pencil. As much as she hated to admit it, Jessica was right—some of the evidence pointed to Robert, but not all of it. The question of motive remained elusive. What drove him to start killing? Why did he choose some of his victims? How did it all add up?

There was something very strange about the whole family, not just Robert, Elizabeth mused.

She'd sensed it at Pembroke Manor; the ancient house on the wild, barren moors reeked of secret passions, secret histories.

Elizabeth flipped back to the first few pages, rereading the notes she'd scribbled at Pembroke Manor, when the entire household was in disarray following the murder of Joy Singleton. After the local police interviewed family members, guests, and servants, Elizabeth had conducted some interviews of her own. *What did I learn, though?* she thought now, frustrated. *Nothing. A big zero, zip, zilch.*

Turning another page, a brief notation caught her eye. "All my love, Annabelle." Elizabeth squinted at the words, remembering their source. *Lord Pembroke's secret library—I copied that inscription from the flyleaf of a book about were-wolves.*

She'd had no idea what to make of it then, and still didn't know if it possessed any significance. *But there's always a chance,* Elizabeth realized. *Who was Annabelle? Could she play a part in the mystery somehow?*

As she stared down at the note, a sudden, powerful hunch swept over Elizabeth. Annabelle was someone important. Annabelle might even hold the key. *All my love, Annabelle . . .*

"I've got to find her," Elizabeth said out loud. "Whoever she is, wherever she is, I bet she knows things about the Pembrokes that no one else does.

She might even be able to lead me to Robert!"

Jumping to her feet, Elizabeth stuck the note-book in her purse and reached for her sweater. It was time to make another visit to Pembroke Manor and the secret library. The answer was there—Elizabeth felt sure of it.

Chapter 8

And it's the perfect time to drop in at Pembroke Manor, Elizabeth reflected as she slipped a new cassette into her mini-corder. *Lord and Lady Pembroke are both in the city, which means only servants are at the country estate. I shouldn't have any problem talking my way into the house.*

After gathering her things together, she started instinctively in the direction of Luke's desk. Then she stopped, a pensive frown on her face. A week or so ago, Luke would have been psyched about the idea of sleuthing around Pembroke Manor—it wouldn't have occurred to her not to ask him to come along. But now . . .

He's been after me to stop investigating on my own, Elizabeth recalled. *If I tell him where I'm going, he'll just say it's not safe and try to talk me out of it. And he'd have a point*, Elizabeth had to acknowledge. The werewolf had already killed twice at Pembroke Manor. . . .

"But I have to go," Elizabeth murmured to herself. "Luke or no Luke."

Since this whole frightening drama had begun, she and Luke had shared everything with each other. She felt somewhat guilty leaving him out of her confidence. *It's for the best,* Elizabeth told herself. *I'll tell him about it afterward, when I've come back in one piece with some great new evidence. Then he'll have to admit I can take care of myself.*

So, it was settled: for the time being, Luke would remain in the dark about her plans to journey to Pembroke Manor. But she should tell someone where she was going, Elizabeth decided. Just in case . . .

Tony was a natural choice, as she needed his permission to take off from work anyhow. Elizabeth stepped over to the cubicle where Tony, a pencil stuck behind his ear, sat typing rapidly on his computer. "Hi, Tony, I wonder if—"

"Liz, there you are," he said, without looking up from the screen. "I have an assignment you might enjoy, a rather racy case of blackmail. I thought we could ah—ah—achew!"

The sneeze sent the pencil flying. Tony reached for a box of tissues. "Darn this cold," he muttered, blowing his nose with a loud honk. "What was I saying?"

"Something about a blackmail story, but I—"

"Oh, yes. I can get you an interview with the—" Tony cut his sentence short, holding up one hand in anticipation of another big sneeze.

Elizabeth took advantage of his momentary silence. "Actually, if you give me the green light, I already have a project in mind that will take the rest of the day," she said quickly. "I want to take the train to Pembroke Woods in order to . . ."

She told him about her Annabelle hunch. The sneeze on hold for the moment, Tony nodded, his watery eyes sparkling with interest. "By all means, we must go to Pembroke Manor," he agreed heartily.

Elizabeth raised her eyebrows. "We?"

"You shouldn't go alone, and two sleuths are better than one."

"What about your cold?" Elizabeth asked. "What about the blackmail case?"

"The blackmail case can wait," said Tony, grabbing a handful of tissues and stuffing them into his pockets. "And since when was a runny nose an excuse not to get a story? It wouldn't stop Adam Silver of the *London Daily Post*. Let's go!"

Lord Pembroke had dozed off. Carefully, Jessica removed her hand from his. Rising to her feet, she tiptoed from the room, easing the door closed behind her.

Tidbits from her strange, half-coherent conversation with Lord Pembroke buzzed through her brain like a swarm of excited bees. *Lord Pembroke is in love with a woman named Annabelle!* Jessica mused. *And Robert has a half brother he doesn't know about, Lord Pembroke's illegitimate son with Annabelle, I bet.* And Annabelle had a pendant similar to the one Jessica wore, which belonged originally to Luke Shepherd's mother, whose name was Ann, not Annabelle. Then there was the file she'd stolen from Dr. Neville's, and which someone else had stolen from her. Could Lord Pembroke's Annabelle be Annabelle S., who years ago died of pneumonia while under Dr. Neville's care? *She could be dead,* thought Jessica. *After all, Lord Pembroke called her "my poor Annabelle."*

Portia had hypothesized that Dr. Neville might have omitted Annabelle's full name from his records in order to preserve her anonymity because she was having an affair. *An affair with Lord Pembroke, Neville's best friend!* Jessica concluded. *It fits. That's what best friends are good for, keeping secrets.*

It wasn't hard to weave the fragments into a compelling story, but Jessica knew she was far from able to prove the truth of any of it, and far, also, from understanding what light the existence of Annabelle—living or dead—and her son might cast on what was happening now.

Lord Pembroke's Annabelle might not be the same as Dr. Neville's, Jessica thought as she strolled back toward the visitors' lounge. She could be alive—the affair could be going on now. Robert's brother might be a little kid, or even a baby.

She needed to know more, that was obvious. But Lord Pembroke had looked pretty ghastly. What if he died and she didn't get another chance to talk to him? There was one other person who might know something about Annabelle. . . .

Jessica peeked into the lounge. Lady Pembroke sat with her coat on, a Styrofoam cup of coffee in one gloved hand. *Tread carefully,* Jessica counseled herself as she stepped into the room. *Don't go blurting stuff out about Lord Pembroke's mistress. Lady P. might not even know about Annabelle. You don't want to scare her off.*

Jessica hesitated, then cleared her throat. "Hello, Lady Pembroke. I see you're about to leave, but I wondered if we could talk for a minute—"

Lady Pembroke glanced up, startled. "What are you doing here, you hateful, nosy American girl?" she cried shrilly.

Jessica blushed. "Well, I heard about Lord Pembroke's . . . accident," she stammered. "I wanted to pay my—"

"You have absolutely no right. You have no place here. Sticking your nose in where you don't belong . . . You're shameless, absolutely shameless!"

Jessica bit her lip. She couldn't blame Lady Pembroke for being so infuriated. *If only Liz hadn't barged in on her that time at Pembroke Green,* she thought, *pretending to be me so she could snoop around for clues . . .*

127

"Lady Pembroke, I know how hard all this is on you, how much stress you're under. I only wanted to—"

"To what?" Lady Pembroke snapped, her pale blue eyes flashing. "To intrude on my privacy? To satisfy your vulgar American curiosity—to gawk at an ancient, distinguished family falling to ruin?"

"It's not like that," Jessica said quietly. "I'm here because I'm truly concerned about Lord Pembroke, and about Robert."

At the mention of her son's name, what was left of Lady Pembroke's shattered composure crumbled into dust. Dropping her coffee cup on the floor, she rose to her feet, swaying slightly. "You were never any good for my son—all you did from the start was stir up trouble," she croaked hoarsely. "I don't ever want to speak to or lay eyes on you again. Clifford!" She clapped her gloved hands together imperiously. "Clifford!"

The family chauffeur materialized out of nowhere and solicitously offered Lady Pembroke his arm. "Take me home," she commanded.

With a swift, sympathetic glance at Jessica, Clifford ushered Lady Pembroke away. Jessica stood looking after them, remembering her high, glorious hopes when she first met Robert . . . and fell for him like a ton of bricks. She'd never forget their first date, when Clifford whisked them in a black limousine all over London. *I wanted so much to make a good impression on Lord and Lady*

Pembroke, Jessica thought sadly. *I wanted them to like me, to love me like a daughter.*

Instead, Lady Pembroke hated her with a passion that didn't appear likely to fade. In her relations with the Pembrokes—and in her attempt to fathom the mystery of Lord Pembroke's affair with Annabelle—Jessica had hit a dead end.

Tickets in hand, Elizabeth and Tony plunged into the sea of people at Victoria Station. "Our train leaves from track eleven in five minutes," Tony shouted. "We'd better hurry!"

Dodging around a large woman with an even larger suitcase, Elizabeth did her best to stay right behind Tony. For half a minute or so, she scrambled along, her eyes fixed on the back of a sandy-haired head and a tweed jacket. Then she realized something. Tony was wearing brown pants, not gray pants, and he wasn't that tall. She was following the wrong guy.

Halting, Elizabeth craned her neck, searching the crowd for her boss. "I'd better just get to the train," she decided. "If I miss it, I'm sunk!"

She hurried forward, her eyes still roving in hopes of spotting Tony. *It's hopeless,* she thought. *Tony is so typically English—half the men here have sandy hair and tweed jackets!* Then her eye was caught by someone who didn't blend into the scene quite so easily—a tall, dark-haired young man in a European-style double-

129

breasted sports coat. Elizabeth blinked. *Rene?*

She stood on tiptoes and waved, trying to catch his eye. The young man didn't look in her direction, however; instead, he turned away and disappeared into the crowd.

Elizabeth shook her head as she trotted on. It must not have been him. What would Rene be doing at Victoria Station in the middle of a workday anyhow? *I probably just imagined I saw him because he's on my mind,* she decided, *because I keep thinking about how I'm always blowing him off.* From the moment she arrived at HIS, Rene had been so happy to resume their acquaintance, so attentive. *I haven't been a very good friend to him in return,* Elizabeth thought with a sigh of regret. She just didn't have the time. It sounded incredibly selfish, but it was true.

Tony was waiting for her at track eleven. "There you are!" he exclaimed with relief. "I thought I'd lost you—I thought I was going to have to figure out the secret door in Pembroke's library by myself."

As the train blew its whistle, an announcement echoed over the loudspeaker. "All aboard for the northwest express to Cauldmoor County. Leaving now, track eleven."

Taking Elizabeth's arm, Tony helped her onto the train. He jumped up behind her just as the doors slid shut. "And we're off," he said, fumbling in his pocket for a tissue. "Ah—ah—achew!"

Jessica sat at her desk at the *Journal*, eating french fries out of a paper bag. It had cheered her up a little to buy lunch at an American-style fast-food restaurant, but only a little.

I'm no Nancy Drew, she acknowledged glumly, squirting ketchup from a foil packet onto her hamburger. Robert was still in hiding somewhere, because he was still the prime suspect, because she hadn't figured out who the real killer was.

She licked her fingers and then fumbled in her shoulder bag for her reporter's notebook. Finding the page where she'd made a list of the werewolf's victims, she added Lord Pembroke's name. Then she scanned the list of possible suspects—people who'd had the opportunity to kill Joy Singleton.

"The servants at Pembroke Manor," Jessica mused aloud. "No, I don't think it's any of them. Most of the attacks have taken place in London— the killer must be based here."

She crossed off the servants. "The chief of police . . . hmm," she murmured. It would be pretty cool if he were the werewolf—just like a "bad cop" movie. Jessica tried the theory on for size. "Lord Pembroke made Thatcher hold off on the police investigation for a while, back when he was trying to protect Robert, even though of course the evidence against Robert is totally trumped up. That was pretty convenient for Thatcher! And it's pretty convenient to have control over the investigation— he can keep steering everybody after Robert, when meanwhile the dead bodies keep piling up."

She bit into her hamburger, pleased with this scenario. "Naturally, he was pretty devastated when he found out his fiancée had been murdered—because he'd meant to kill someone else. Me." A puzzled frown wrinkled her forehead. "Why would he want to kill me, though? Why would he want to kill any of these people? Just for the fun of it?"

She scrawled a question mark next to Andrew Thatcher's name and moved on down the list of suspects. Lady Pembroke. Now, there was an intriguing possibility. "She looked pretty upset at the hospital this morning, but that could have just been an act," Jessica reflected. "Maybe she went after Lord Pembroke herself, to get revenge because he had an affair!"

It was a juicy, workable theory, but it broke down as soon as Jessica pushed it a little further. What about all the other victims—why would Lady Pembroke kill them? And what about Robert? Would Lady Pembroke really just sit by and watch while her only beloved son went to jail in her place?

"Besides, she's too fastidious," Jessica decided. "She wouldn't want to mess up her hair and clothes—she's the type who'd hire someone else to do the dirty work for her."

Jessica gave Lady Pembroke a question mark. "Luke Shepherd." She popped a french fry in her mouth and tried to imagine Elizabeth's moony boyfriend prowling around London after dark and slashing people's throats. She laughed out loud. "Not that he isn't weird," she said with her mouth full. "He'd make a pretty good werewolf because he knows so much about them. And he's a loner, and serial killers are always loners." Still, it didn't jive. "People who write poetry are too wimpy to be murderers," Jessica concluded.

She started to scratch off Luke's name, then stopped herself. *Gotta keep him on the list—he's the easiest one to investigate!* she reasoned.

Wrapping up the rest of her hamburger, Jessica wiped her fingers on a paper napkin and got to her feet. Nonchalantly, she wandered across the office toward Luke's section.

The arts and entertainment staff were all out to lunch, so Jessica marched boldly up to Luke's desk and starting snooping through his stuff.

She found a coffee mug with some old, cold tea in the bottom, a book of English poetry, two half-finished movie reviews, and a handful of paper scraps—notes for stories in progress. *What did you expect?* Jessica asked herself, stifling a giggle. *A confession, signed "The Werewolf"?*

She opened a desk drawer. As she was about to pick up a fat spiral notebook with a red cover, she heard footsteps behind her. "May I help you?" Luke demanded.

Jessica turned, an innocent smile on her face.

"Who, me? Oh, yes. I just wanted to borrow . . . a stapler. Do you have one?"

Luke frowned, and then shrugged. Jessica stepped away from his desk, watching as he opened another drawer and pulled out a stapler. "Will this do?" he asked briskly.

"Thanks," said Jessica, taking the stapler. "I'll bring it back in a sec."

Luke waved her off. "Keep it."

Stapler in hand, Jessica sauntered back to the main newsroom. He definitely acted guilty, she decided. He must be hiding something in that desk. *Yeah, some gooey love poetry—"Ode to Elizabeth."*

Seated at her desk again, Jessica gave Luke a question mark. *I'm making great progress*, she thought sarcastically as she chewed a cold french fry. One question mark after another . . .

Two hours after boarding the train in Victoria Station, Elizabeth and Tony disembarked in the tiny country village of Pembroke Woods. "It's another world, eh?" remarked Tony, eyeing the cobblestone streets and ancient ivy-covered cottages.

"Another century," said Elizabeth. She felt the same way she had the first time she came to Pembroke Woods, as if she'd been transported back in time. "Robert told us those weavers' cottages were built four hundred years ago."

"And the town hasn't changed a whit since, I wager," said Tony. He gestured to a weathered

134

wooden sign. "I'll find out from the tavern-keeper whether they run to such modern conveniences as taxicabs."

Tony ducked into the White Swan Inn and Elizabeth wandered onto a rickety wooden bridge. A pair of the majestic swans that gave the inn its name floated in the crystal-clear brook below, their dirty-gray cygnets paddling single file after them. It was hard to believe, Elizabeth thought, that two people were recently murdered just a few miles from this tranquil spot.

Turning back, Elizabeth saw Tony emerge from the inn, a heavyset farmer with a round, sunburnt face lumbering after him. "The bad news is, the town's one taxi is in the shop for repairs," Tony reported. "The good news is, this kind gentleman has offered to run us up to Pembroke Manor in his . . . conveyance."

The farmer's "conveyance" turned out to be a dilapidated pickup truck filled with grimy farm tools and dusty hay. Tony had a sneezing fit the instant he climbed in. "We should have skipped the train and hired a car in the city!" Tony hollered as the pickup rattled along a bumpy country road, he and Elizabeth bouncing around in the back.

The wind whipped Elizabeth's hair. "This makes it more of an adventure!"

The sensation of entering another world increased as they drove deeper into the woods outside the village. Elizabeth pointed out the ruins of

Woodleigh Abbey through the trees. "Haunted," she yelled to Tony.

"I believe it," he yelled back, tucking his chin down into the collar of his jacket.

There was one brief delay as the farmer stopped to let a flock of sheep meander across the road. Soon after, the truck crested a hill and Pembroke Manor appeared below them.

Elizabeth caught her breath, just as she had at her first sight of the stately fieldstone house built around an enormous emerald-green courtyard. With the rugged moors in the distance, it looked like the setting for a gothic novel.

At the top of the driveway, the farmer braked. "This is as far as I go," he called out the window to his passengers. "The family's nowt but bad luck lately. There's something gone wrong with that house and everyone in it. I'd be careful if I were you."

Tony and Elizabeth hopped down. Pulling a U-turn, the farmer sped off in a cloud of dust.

Together, the two faced Pembroke Manor. *There's no going back*, Elizabeth thought, taking a deep breath and starting forward.

"That was easier than I thought it would be," she whispered to Tony as they walked along the lofty, cathedral-like hall of Pembroke Manor toward the library.

"You heard that farmer—with a family member suspected of being a serial killer, the Pembrokes are probably having a tough time holding on to their help," said Tony. "It's a magnificent house, but it's acquiring a gruesome reputation. Can't say I'd want to spend a night under this roof!"

"Me, either," agreed Elizabeth. "Never again."

"What a fine collection of old books," Tony said as they entered Lord Pembroke's library, a typically English and very masculine room decorated with burgundy leather furniture and heavy brocade curtains.

Elizabeth stepped around the massive mahogany desk. "Watch this!"

As Tony watched in astonishment, she reached for a book on one of the shelves—a leatherbound edition of Robert Louis Stevenson's *The Strange Case of Dr. Jekyll and Mr. Hyde*. As she slowly removed the volume, a panel in the adjacent wall swung open to reveal a hidden door.

Tony's eyes nearly popped out of his head. "My, look at that! Just like in the films!"

Elizabeth slipped into the shadowy secret room, Tony following close behind her. She flipped on a light switch and he whistled. "Good heavens. I see why you've been calling it the wolf den!"

The walls of the small room were draped with wild animal skins and mounted trophy heads, mostly of wolves. "And all the books are about werewolves," Elizabeth told Tony. "It's Lord Pembroke Senior's big hobby."

"An obsession, more like," said Tony. "Robert must have known of this place, wouldn't you say?

He must have read some of these books—absorbed the lore. This is where he learned what kind of killer he wanted to become."

Elizabeth nodded. "It's a good theory. Here's the book from Annabelle." Taking it from the shelf, she offered it for Tony's inspection. "*Discours de la Lyncanthropie*—it's in French, from the sixteenth century. See?"

Tony read the inscription. "Well, let's get to work and see what else we can find."

Starting at opposite sides of the study, they began methodically examining each and every volume on the shelves. "Here's another one given to him by Annabelle!" Elizabeth cried after five minutes.

"Anything special about it?" asked Tony.

Elizabeth flipped through the pages. "Not particularly," she admitted, putting it back.

Twenty minutes later, they were nearly ready to give up. "We haven't learned anything new about Annabelle," declared Elizabeth, frustrated. "She gave Lord P. half a dozen books about werewolves, so we can conclude she was as interested in them as he was. But what kind of relationship did they have? Who was she?"

Tony shook his head. "She's a mystery woman."

"Well, let's get through these last two shelves," suggested Elizabeth. "Then we can look around some more in the big library."

Starting in on a new shelf, she looked at four books. Nothing. But there was something odd about the fifth book. *It's so light,* Elizabeth thought, weighing it in her hand. *It's almost as if it's . . .*

"Look!" she squealed. "This one's hollow—it's not really a book at all! It's a box that looks like a book." She lifted the front cover, the box's lid. "Something's inside." Her eyes widened with the thrill of discovery. "Letters!"

Eagerly, she removed a sheaf of old, faded letters from the box. Tony looked over her shoulder. "Don't tell me they're from—" he began.

Elizabeth glanced at the signature on the top letter. "Annabelle!" she confirmed excitedly.

They sat down cross-legged on the floor, the correspondence spread out before them, and each took a letter. As she read, Elizabeth's eyes grew rounder and rounder. The letter she'd chosen started, "My beloved Robert, I miss you more than I can say. It is such agony to be apart at a time like this. When can we be together?"

"They're love letters," Elizabeth gasped.

Tony nodded. "I'll say! And they go way back. This is twenty years old."

Elizabeth picked up another sheet of pale-pink paper covered with faded, graceful script. "This one is more recent, written only ten years ago."

"It must have been quite a love affair," remarked Tony.

"And quite a friendship," said Elizabeth, skimming a letter. "It's not all romantic stuff. Here she

139

writes for a whole page about books she's read, and then for a page more about politics."

"Look at this one—I think it's the most recent."

Tony handed a letter to Elizabeth. It was dated just nine years ago. "Dear R.," it began simply. "I haven't much strength, so this will be brief. I haven't much time. . . . The doctor, your dear friend, is cheerful as always, but I see the truth in his eyes, and feel it in my heart. Pain and loneliness press down on me until I pray that I'll fall asleep and slip peacefully away—if only it didn't mean leaving my precious child, and you, my only love. How it hurts, more than any illness, to know I'll never see your face again! Forget me, Robert— it will be best. But take care of our son. I've never asked anything of you, and never will again, so please do just this one thing. . . ."

Elizabeth looked up from the letter, her eyes damp with sentimental tears. "Wow. They had a child together, and then she must have died. It's like a movie or something." Suddenly, something came together in her mind with an almost audible click. "The family scandal! Eliana couldn't remember what it was about, exactly, only that it took place a long time ago."

"Perhaps Lady Pembroke found out about the affair," deduced Tony. "I bet Annabelle's husband did, anyway. She doesn't mention him in the last batch of letters—he probably left her."

Elizabeth glanced down at the sheet of stationery. The words Annabelle had written so long ago seemed to jump off the page, to breathe with affection and vitality. *You, my only love . . .*

"They were so in love," she said as she copied the return address from one of the envelopes into her notebook. "And it was real. It lasted years and years. Why didn't they marry each other?"

"Love doesn't count for much in matters like these, especially with the aristocracy," Tony said, somewhat heartlessly, Elizabeth thought. "In this instance, clearly it wasn't enough to overcome the obstacle of class."

"Class? What do you mean?"

"Well, it's apparent from her letters that although Annabelle was extremely well-read and intelligent, she and Pembroke were of a different social status. It sounds like her husband was a shopkeeper of some sort, and here"—he pointed to one of the letters—"she writes about having to cut short a family holiday to the seaside because of financial constraints. I know it strikes a romantic American like you as odd, perhaps even despicable, but our class distinctions have long formed the basis of English civilization. The prince only marries the flower girl in fairy tales, or Hollywood movies. Knowing Lord Pembroke, that's why he wouldn't leave Lady Pembroke for Annabelle."

"Wow," Elizabeth said again. "It's so tragic. Poor Annabelle. And her little son—what do you think happened to him?" She clapped a hand

141

over her mouth. "You don't suppose it's—"

"Little Lord Pembroke?" Tony shook his head. "No. Lady Pembroke would never have allowed her husband to raise the result of an adulterous affair in her home as her son. No, Annabelle and Lord Robert's progeny, who would be anywhere from nine to nineteen, is probably in an orphanage or on the street."

On the street . . . Elizabeth remembered the homeless man Sergeant Bumpo had carted off the day before. Her heart ached for the abandoned child, perhaps homeless himself, and the star-crossed lovers who had been his parents.

"We discovered the secret of Annabelle," Elizabeth said softly, holding the letters for a moment before returning them to their hiding place. "But this is all she's going to tell us."

Annabelle had long been silent. They'd reached a dead end.

"Ten minutes—grand," Tony said into the phone back in the main library. "We'll meet you in the drive." Hanging up, he turned to watch as Elizabeth pushed the Robert Louis Stevenson volume back into place and the trick panel swung shut, sealing off the secret room. "The town taxi is back in service and on its way to collect us."

"I guess Annabelle didn't turn out to be the key to the mystery," Elizabeth reflected as she and Tony headed back toward the entrance to the manor.

"Actually, maybe she is." Tony's eyes sparkled with inspiration. "Imagine it this way. Robert at some point discovered the werewolf room. Any boy or young man would be fascinated by such a place—he went there secretly to read the scary werewolf books. And one day . . . he does what you did. He picks the fake book from the shelf and discovers the love letters!"

"And so . . . ?"

"Perhaps finding out about Lord Pembroke's affair led to Robert's killing spree somehow. Perhaps Robert became unbalanced, fearing he might lose his inheritance or have to share it with Annabelle's son, or just from knowing what his father had done."

Elizabeth pondered this theory. "It could have happened that way," she conceded. "But it still doesn't explain everything, like why he chose some of his victims."

"If he chose at all," Tony pointed out. "Maybe he just snapped."

The main entry hall was deserted. Elizabeth and Tony paused there for a moment to look up at a large, ancient tapestry hanging on one of the stone walls. "The Pembroke family crest," Elizabeth told Tony. She pointed to the wolf in one of the shield's quadrants. "And guess what woodland creature happens to be the Pembrokes' patron saint?"

"Ironic, isn't it?" said Tony.

While they'd searched the secret room and perused Annabelle's letters, the sun had set. "The cab's not here yet," Tony observed, peering into the night. "I certainly hope it hasn't broken down again! Let's hope for the best and walk out to the main road to meet it, shall we?"

Elizabeth nodded reluctantly. On the one hand, she was glad to get out of Pembroke Manor; she was sure the old house was full of ghosts. But the inky darkness of the English countryside was hardly more comforting. The full moon that had been out the weekend she, Jessica, and Luke visited Pembroke Manor had been eerie and foreboding . . . and for Joy Singleton, fatal. Elizabeth shivered. *But this moonless gloom is almost worse. . . .*

They walked down the driveway without speaking, their feet crunching on the gravel. A light breeze stirred the leaves.

"What's that?" Elizabeth cried, stopping abruptly in her tracks.

"What's what?" Tony asked.

Her heart thumping, Elizabeth stood still as a statue and listened. There was nothing but the whispering of the trees. "I—I thought I heard something," she said apologetically. "I'm just a little jumpy, I guess."

"That makes two of us," Tony muttered, striding on.

Elizabeth trotted along next to him, her eyes darting from side to side. *Is that a person,* she thought, glimpsing a movement in the dark woods, *or just a tree shadow?*

She decided that, if she didn't want to keel over from fright, her best bet was to look straight ahead and walk as fast as she could. Which she did. But her skin continued to prickle, and logical or illogical, she was gripped by a disconcerting sensation that was starting to become familiar. She'd been getting it off and on all week. *Someone is out there in the dark and he's following me. . . .*

He watched the girl and the man from the shadowy woods. Snuffling the damp leaves and earth, he prowled closer to the edge of the trees. The two were alone and vulnerable, far from any human habitation. No one would hear them cry out. And if he dragged their bodies into the woods, chances were good they wouldn't be found for days or even weeks.

He rose to his full height, his muscles bunched and his jaw aching with the desire to rip and tear, to taste blood. He prepared to spring . . . and then dropped back down onto all fours, drawing back into the gloom.

No, now is not the time. There were two of them, and as the moon wasn't full, he wasn't at his full strength. *They are watching for me, hunting me, closing in. . . .*

But he wasn't cornered yet. He was still free, and he, too, was closer than ever to his goal.

The Wakefield girl and her companion disappeared around a bend in the drive and he loped toward the manor. The stately house towered above him, dark except for a few lights in the servants' quarters.

Stealing inside, he trailed the scent of the two visitors along the hallway, which was lit now by candles guttering in wall sconces. On noiseless feet, he padded into the library, sniffing. *They were here. . . .*

Triggering the secret panel, he entered the werewolf study. *And here . . .*

He stood before the bookcase where Elizabeth had stood, and reached where she had reached. The fake book fell open in his clawed hand, revealing the packet of letters within. Lifting them reverently, he breathed the fragile, faded perfume of the woman who wrote them long ago and, lifting his head, howled balefully into the night.

Chapter 9

Jessica trudged dejectedly up the steps to the front door of HIS. Crossing the foyer, she paused at the bottom of the stairs and then started up, leaning on the banister with all her weight. She felt listless and spent; it was all she could do to lift one foot after the other. *I just want to sleep,* she thought sadly, *and wake up and be back in sunny Sweet Valley with all of this a crazy, terrible dream.*

Portia was knotting a silk scarf around her neck as Jessica shuffled into their bedroom and flung herself on the bottom bunk. "Look what the cat dragged in," said Portia. "Busy day at the newspaper, eh?"

"Umm," Jessica mumbled, rolling onto her back and closing her eyes.

Portia swept a brush through her cascading dark hair. "I'm running a bit late for the theater,

147

but I have a minute for supper. Join me for a bite downstairs?"

Jessica shook her head. "I'm too depressed to eat."

Portia sat down on the bed next to her. "Poor girl. What is it now?"

"Didn't you hear the news today?" asked Jessica. "Lord Pembroke was attacked by the werewolf!"

"No," Portia gasped. "How awful!"

"He survived, but he's at death's door. I visited him in the hospital and he looked horrible, but he was conscious and he recognized me. And he said the wildest things. He talked about someone named Annabelle."

"Annabelle. Like the name on the file you pinched from the dead doctor's office!" Portia exclaimed.

"Maybe. I don't know if she's the same," said Jessica. "But whoever she is, she and Lord P. had an affair—maybe they're still having one. And they had a kid. Robert has an illegitimate half brother somewhere!"

"Unbelievable. You're sure of all this?"

"The conversation was kind of sketchy and disjointed, and Lord Pembroke was pretty heavily sedated." Jessica sighed. "I don't know, maybe none of it's even true. Maybe he was just delirious."

Portia shook her head. "No, it's more likely that the truth would come out at a moment like that. What a shock, and how intriguing!"

Jessica sat up, propping her back against some pillows. "I can't help feeling that somehow this secret is really important, that it has something to do with the killings," she said, a measure of energy returning. "Robert's innocent—he would never hurt his father. But that means someone else is guilty, most likely someone connected to the Pembrokes somehow. Finding out about this other family breaks the whole thing wide open—there's a whole new direction."

"You need to learn more about Annabelle and her son," Portia agreed.

"After I saw Lord P., I tried to talk to Lady P. You know, just sound her out a bit. But she blew me off completely—she thinks I'm just looking to make trouble." Jessica punched the mattress, frustrated. "But she knows something, I'm sure she does. She could help me, she could help her son, if only she'd stop hiding her head in the sand. She'll never agree to see me, though—she's the most stubborn woman on earth."

Portia tipped her head to one side. "There must be a way we could break through her defenses," she mused. "Vain, self-important Lady Henrietta Pembroke . . ." Portia's gray eyes glinted with mischief. "I have an idea."

"What?"

Portia shook her head, smiling. "I'll tell you later, after I make sure we can pull it off." Rising, she slipped on a butter-soft black leather jacket and headed for the door. "Now I'm late in earnest—I'll have to go onstage without makeup at this rate!"

"Break a leg," Jessica called after her.

Portia stepped into the hallway and then turned back. "One other thing. You really should have some supper—you need to keep up your strength. And there's going to be a surprise in the dining room this evening."

"A surprise?" Despite her gloom, Jessica perked up. "What is it?"

But Portia had left. Jessica was alone.

For fifteen minutes, Jessica lay on her bed thinking hard about the Pembrokes. Finally, she stood up with a sigh. *I can't solve anything without more information. And if I don't get something to eat soon, I'm going to pass out.*

A surprise for dinner—wonder what it is? she thought as she thumped downstairs. *Something yummy for dessert, maybe.*

She entered the foyer just as the front door swung open. Elizabeth appeared, her cheeks flushed and her hair damp from the evening mist. Jessica bit back the question that jumped to her lips, even though she was dying to ask it. *Where were you all afternoon?*

Her chin in the air, Jessica breezed past Elizabeth into the dining room. She could hear her sister marching right behind her. *But I got here first,* Jessica thought maliciously. *I'll get to sit with Em and David and Gabe and she'll have to sit in the corner by herself. Ha!*

But as the twins appeared in the doorway, the

"surprise" jumped up and ran toward them. "Jessica! Elizabeth! It's so nice to see you!"

"Eliana!" Jessica and Elizabeth both exclaimed.

Their former dorm roommate, Princess Eliana, hugged each sister in turn, smiling radiantly. "I just had to come back for a visit. I really miss the old place!"

Taking Jessica with one arm and Elizabeth with the other, Eliana led them over to the table where Emily, Gabriello, and David were sitting. "Isn't this jolly?" Eliana declared. "Just like the good old days. Oh, I wish you could all live at the palace with me—wouldn't we have fun!"

"Sit, sit," Emily urged.

The three sat down, Jessica and Elizabeth facing each other across the table. "Doesn't she look great?" Emily asked the twins.

"I don't know," said David, smiling shyly. "I kind of miss the glasses and mousy brown hair."

Eliana tossed her pale blond hair, laughing. "Don't tease me," she begged. "I haven't gotten over worrying that you liked me better as Lina Smith."

"Eliana, what brings you to this neighborhood?" asked Elizabeth.

"Emily phoned to ask me over, and I just snuck off," said Eliana. When she saw Elizabeth's look, she laughed again. "Oh, I didn't sneak, literally. My running away days are over. This is part of my new freedom—I come and go as I please."

"With security guards and chauffeurs in tow, of course," remarked Gabriello.

"A fact of my life," Eliana conceded.

"So . . . Emily phoned you," said Elizabeth. She was smiling at Eliana with sincere warmth, but Jessica didn't need her twin intuition to pick up on a distinct sense of annoyance. *Liz sees right through this gimmick, too. They're trying to get us to make up. They knew we'd have to sit together, maybe even talk to each other, if Eliana came over.*

Freckle-faced Emily was the picture of innocence. "We were overdue for a reunion, don't you think?"

Jessica folded her arms across her chest and pushed out her lower lip, refusing to be manipulated.

Elizabeth shrugged. "Sure."

"So, these guys have filled me in on their exciting lives. Tell me what you've been up to," Eliana said to Jessica and Elizabeth. "How is the scene at the *London Journal*? What exciting story did you investigate today?"

Jessica looked at Elizabeth, waiting for her answer. Elizabeth toyed with her napkin. "I was out of the office most of the day, doing some . . . independent research," she mumbled.

"That sounds interesting," Eliana remarked. "What kind of independent research?"

"Yes, Liz, do tell us all about it," Jessica snapped, unable to restrain herself. "Were you snooping around the Pembrokes again, pretending to be me? Did you dig up some new dirt, find some new ways to trap and incriminate Robert?"

Elizabeth flushed a hot, angry red. "What about you? Where did you disappear to? Do you know where Robert's hiding—did you meet him someplace? How much longer are you planning to protect him, Jessica? Till he goes to the gas chamber as a convicted murderer?"

Jessica turned pale. Emily, David, and Gabriello looked shocked.

Eliana clapped her hands. "Elizabeth! Girls, please. This just won't do!"

"No, it won't." Jessica shoved back her chair and stood up. "Nice try, Eliana, but you can't order us around like the servants at Buckingham Palace. Don't you see why it won't work? Didn't you hear her? Well, I for one won't listen to garbage like that, but I guess the rest of you agree with her." Jessica glared tearfully at her friends, or the people she thought were her friends. In her whole life, she'd never been so angry; she'd never felt so hurt, so isolated. "I hate you, Elizabeth," she sobbed. "I hate you all!"

"I wish you'd go upstairs and say something to her," Eliana begged Elizabeth as they sat in the HIS library after dinner. "Anything, just a word or two. Tell her you're sorry and then leave her alone to get a grip on herself."

"Tell her I'm sorry?" Elizabeth scoffed. "For what? She's so unreasonable and ungrateful. Everything I've been doing, I've been doing for her. I'm trying to help solve this case so she'll be safe—so we'll all be safe. It's not my fault if she won't see that."

Eliana sighed, her bright blue eyes troubled. "I just hate. seeing you feuding so bitterly at a time like this. I had such confidence that I'd be able to bring you back together, and now my hopes are dashed."

Elizabeth's expression softened. "You're sweet to care so much, Lina. Don't take what Jessica said too much to heart. She hates me, but she doesn't really hate you, and you should visit her again. Just don't," she added, "try to visit us both at the same time."

Eliana squeezed Elizabeth's hand and then stood up. "I won't give up that easily," she said with a smile. "I'm used to having things go my way. I'm a princess, remember!"

The royal limousine was parked in front of the dorm, its engine running. David joined Elizabeth and Eliana in the foyer. "I'll walk you out," he offered Eliana.

Eliana took David's hand, and with her other hand, blew a good-bye kiss to Elizabeth. Standing in the doorway, Elizabeth waved after them.

Just like the good old days—hardly, Elizabeth thought, turning away with a melancholy sigh. It was nice to see Eliana, but it wasn't the same when she was whisked in and out in royal fashion. It wasn't the same as when they were roommates, and could stay up late every night gabbing.

Elizabeth wandered back to the deserted library. The entire dorm seemed unnaturally quiet. *David has gone off with Eliana, Emily's cheering up Jessica, Gabriello is studying in his room,* Elizabeth thought, swamped by a sudden wave of loneliness. *There's absolutely no one to talk to.*

Or maybe there was. Walking upstairs, she paused on the second-floor landing. Mrs. Bates had strict rules: no girls on the boys' floor, no boys on the girls' floor. Elizabeth glanced over her shoulder. *Just this once . . . what are the odds I'll get caught? And so what if I do? Who really cares?*

Tiptoeing down the hall, she knocked softly on Rene's door. "Rene, psst!" she hissed. "It's Liz. Open up!"

She waited, but there was no response. She tried the doorknob: locked.

With a discouraged sigh, Elizabeth stomped back toward the stairs. "So much for Rene supposedly wanting so badly to be my friend," she grumbled to herself. "I can't believe I actually wasted time feeling guilty because we weren't seeing much of each other! He keeps spouting off about how worried he is about me, but from day one, he's always been too busy at the embassy to think of anything or anyone else."

155

No, he's never around when the chips are down, Elizabeth concluded. *He just shows up after the fact acting gallant and making promises he can't keep. Good thing I'm not counting on him to look out for me!*

Jessica was asleep when Elizabeth tiptoed into the dark bedroom at eleven o'clock. She undressed quietly, her teeth chattering as she slipped her flannel nightgown over her head; one of the windows was open a crack and a cold draft of very unsummerlike air brushed her bare skin like icy fingers.

Diving into bed, Elizabeth pulled the covers up to her nose, curling her body into a ball. Gradually, she started to warm up. *I'll never get used to this English weather,* she thought as she lay listening to the sound of rain pattering on the windowpane. Closing her eyes, she conjured up a vision of a balmy, fragrant summer night in Sweet Valley. She and Todd were walking barefoot on the beach in the moonlight, holding hands. *In just a few more weeks,* she thought.

The vision was as fragile as a candle flame in the wind. When Elizabeth opened her eyes again, it disappeared as if it had never existed—as if there were no such place as Sweet Valley, California, no such boy as Todd Wilkins, no such girl as Elizabeth Wakefield had been before she came to England to intern for the *London Journal*.

The only thing that was real was the present:

where she was now, who she was now. She was in London, a city terrorized by a brutal, demonic serial killer. She was trying to solve the mystery, to track the werewolf to his lair, without losing her own life in the process.

Propping herself up on one elbow, Elizabeth reached for her purse, which was on top of the bedside table. Taking out her notebook, she turned to the last note she'd made that afternoon at Pembroke Manor.

It was the return address she'd copied from the envelope of one of Annabelle's love letters to Lord Pembroke: A.C.S., Four Forget-Me-Not Lane.

Forget-Me-Not Lane—how appropriate, Elizabeth mused. Did Lord Pembroke think of her still? Did he look after their son as she asked on her deathbed? Did he store her letters in that box to keep them close at hand so he could read them, or was he hiding them away, out of sight and out of mind, forever?

Elizabeth tucked the notebook back in her purse and rested her head on the cool pillow. Her wide, sleepless eyes fixed on the dark window, she watched the raindrops streak down the glass. A gust of air, soft as a ghostly breath, lifted the curtain. It was as if the whole city sighed in sorrow for the lives that had been lost, Elizabeth thought fancifully. And somewhere, a murderer continued to prowl the black, rain-slick streets. . . .

"Annabelle," Elizabeth whispered. "If only you

were alive. Could you help me understand what happened to the Pembroke family? Could you tell me where Robert is, and why he's done what he's done?"

Jessica tossed in her sleep, caught in the grip of a dream in which she was running down the streets of London in the night, but whether running toward something or away from something, she wasn't sure. And now, from somewhere outside the dream, a voice called out to her, trying to wake her. *Annabelle*, the voice whispered. *Annabelle*.

Jessica's lips moved; her eyelids fluttered, but remained closed. In her dream, she stopped and stood on the sidewalk, peering around her into the fog. "Where are you, Annabelle?" Jessica asked in her dream. "Annabelle, is that you?"

Ahead, the fog thinned and the figure of a woman in a flowing white gown materialized. Jessica couldn't distinguish her features or even the color of her hair; still, she could see that the woman beckoned to her, inviting her to follow.

But before Jessica could take even one step forward, the woman disappeared, melting into the mist. Or was she just a wisp of fog all along, never really there at all?

"Annabelle!" Jessica called hopelessly. "Annabelle, where is your son? Do you know, Annabelle? Do you know who the werewolf is? Annabelle! Annabelle!"

In her dream, Jessica ran on into the night, her hands held out, hoping to grasp hold of Annabelle and her secrets, as all around her the fog echoed with the sound of a wild animal howling, a sound that drew closer and closer. . . .

Chapter 10

At the *Journal* offices Wednesday morning, Elizabeth hurried straight to Tony's desk to see what he thought of the idea of going to Forget-Me-Not Lane, even though of course Annabelle didn't live there anymore, having died years ago.

She found Tony standing at ironic attention with a box of tissues in his hand while the editor-in-chief, one hip perched on the edge of his desk, delivered a peppery lecture on the importance of timeliness in journalism.

"Let me get this straight," said Lucy, tossing back her long chestnut hair. "The blackmail article that I planned to put on the front page of the second section simply . . . doesn't exist."

"It's not written," Tony admitted cheerfully. "In fact, it's not even begun."

"And why is that, Mr. Crime Editor?" Lucy

crossed her arms. "What's been going on in this department since I left it?"

"Oh, lots," said Tony. Holding a tissue to his nose, he sneezed vigorously. "Achew! In fact, we have a whole new attitude toward reporting crime."

"I bet," said Lucy sarcastically. "Let me see. You imagine a fresh new focus on the subject, perhaps an angle inspired by your sojourn on the society page."

Tony cocked a finger, grinning. "How about, 'Hemlines, Hairstyles, and Homicide: The Hidden Connection'?"

"Seriously, Frank." Lucy fixed him with a stern glare, but Elizabeth saw her lips twitch. "You're accountable for a big department now and I want to see product. Where were you all day yesterday?"

Tony shot a glance at Elizabeth. "Liz and I were doing some more background work on the Pembrokes for the werewolf story."

Lucy held out her hand. "Let's see what you got."

"We don't know what we've got," Tony explained. "We don't know what it all adds up to yet. But when we do, you'll be the first to see it. You've got to trust us on this, Friday."

Lucy bit her lip. "I'm trusting you—this time. But let's get one thing straight, Frank. If you think you can cover up for substandard work or no work at all by flirting with me, you've got another think coming. A charming smile isn't going to win any

162

journalism prizes . . . and it's not going to guarantee you keep your byline." Standing up, Lucy looked Tony straight in the eye. "Consider this your first and last warning. Don't blow it, Frank."

Lucy strode off, her hair bouncing on her shoulders. Tony stared after her, his eyes glassy. "Wow," he breathed. "She packs a powerful punch, doesn't she?"

"Are you OK?" Elizabeth asked. Tony's face was pale and his skin had a glossy sheen. "You look like you're running a fever."

"The boss has that effect on me," he said with a lopsided grin. "Did you hear that? She thinks I have a charming smile!"

"That's great," said Elizabeth. "But I wanted to ask you about something. What do you think about going to Annabelle's old house, just to see if we can find out anything from the people who live there now, or the neighbors?"

"Let's do it. I'm ready when you are!"

"Since it's not really official business, maybe we should wait until after work," Elizabeth suggested. "Otherwise Lucy might fire us."

"After work—it's a date." Tony blew his nose loudly. "We'll get to the bottom of the Annabelle mystery and find out if it's just a red herring or the key to the story of the century."

"We haven't been here in ages," Elizabeth said to Luke as they entered the Slaughtered Lamb at lunchtime. "Things have been so hectic lately!"

Luke had shared his favorite local pub with Elizabeth the very first day they met. She'd thought the name was creepy at first—there was a Slaughtered Lamb Pub in the movie *An American Werewolf in London*—but the restaurant turned out to be warm and homey and intimate and it had quickly become "their" place. For a while, they'd managed to drop in for lunch or tea nearly every day.

"I missed you yesterday," Luke told Elizabeth as they slid into a booth near the crackling fire. "I kept dropping by your desk, hoping for a chat, but you must have been off chasing a big story. Does Tony have you working on an interesting assignment?"

"Actually . . ." Elizabeth sipped from the mug of hot tea that the waitress had put in front of her. "I was chasing a big story, though it's not really a work assignment. I went back to Pembroke Manor."

Luke's face darkened. "Elizabeth, what were you thinking?" he cried, his blue eyes shooting sparks. "I've warned you that it's not safe. What if something had happened to you? What if—"

"I'm here, aren't I?" Elizabeth reasoned. "No harm came to me. And besides, I wasn't alone— Tony went with me."

Luke relaxed somewhat. "Thank goodness for that." He drew a hand across his forehead, and Elizabeth saw that he was shaking. "What would I have done," he murmured, almost to himself, "if anything had happened to you?"

Reaching out, Elizabeth touched his arm. "Nothing happened to me," she repeated. "I swear, I'm not taking any unnecessary chances." *Not many, anyhow,* she added silently. "And it was worth it. We made an incredible discovery!"

"You did?"

"Yes. We went back to look at the books in the secret werewolf library, to see if any more of them were from Annabelle or if there were any other clues to who she might be."

"Annabelle?" Luke sat forward. "You found books from someone named Annabelle in the werewolf library?"

"I found one the first time I was in there," said Elizabeth, "but I'd completely forgotten about it until I read through my notes yesterday morning. Then it occurred to me that maybe Annabelle was a person it would pay to learn more about."

"And what did you learn?"

"That she had an affair with Lord Pembroke!" Elizabeth revealed. "It lasted for years and years. In fact, they had a child together, a son. Robert's illegitimate half brother."

Luke sucked in his breath. "An affair . . . a son! How on earth did you . . . ?"

"Old love letters from Annabelle to Lord Pembroke—a boxful of them," said Elizabeth. "They told the whole story. Well, Annabelle's side of it, anyway."

"The whole story . . ." Luke raked a hand

165

through his black hair. "What does it mean, though? Do you think there's a connection to the murders? Could Robert know about this? What else did you find?"

He shot the questions at her machine-gun style. Elizabeth blinked at his intensity. "Nothing—we didn't find anything else. And I don't know if there's a connection. It's all still fuzzy and vague."

Elizabeth started to reach for her tea. Luke intercepted her hand, clasping it tightly in his own. "You're taking too many risks, Elizabeth. You mustn't visit the werewolf's haunts—you mustn't go where he might find you. If you were the next victim . . ." His voice cracked with emotion. "I wouldn't be able to bear it. I wouldn't be able to live."

Elizabeth's heart throbbed with pity and affection. Luke had lost someone he loved before—he was so vulnerable. *This isn't the time to tell him about Tony's and my plan to go to Annabelle's this afternoon,* she decided. "I'll be careful, but I won't just sit home," she told Luke, squeezing his hand. "It's too late for that—we've come too far. Don't you feel it? Don't you feel how close we are?"

"Close . . . yes." He nodded, his eyes somber. "Soon, he'll be cornered—we'll confront him, face-to-face. And if we're prepared, if we have the right weapons . . ."

Elizabeth thought about the silver bullet, now lost. Lost . . . or stolen by the werewolf himself?

"We can leave the weapons to the police," she said. "All we have to do is find him." As she and Luke clasped hands across the table, she felt it again, in her bones, in her blood. "And we're close," Elizabeth whispered. "So close . . ."

"I'm done with my work, but I can tell you're not done with yours," Jessica said to Lucy at five thirty Wednesday afternoon. "Should I stick around to help you out?"

Lucy waved a hand without looking up from the editorial she was composing. "I've got it under control. We had a productive day. Go on, get out of here."

Smiling, Jessica turned on her heel and breezed off. *I like that woman,* she thought. *She's gorgeous and smart and tough—she has style. Hey, maybe journalism wouldn't be such a bad career after all!*

It had been a good day, and the best part about it was that she hadn't bumped into Elizabeth once. *And if I never see her again in my life, that'll be too soon.* As she walked outside to the curb and boarded a double-decker bus, Jessica remembered their fight the previous evening at dinner—their worst fight yet. *Worst and last,* she thought. *Because I really, really don't ever plan to speak to her again. Although I do want to see her face when it's finally revealed that somebody else is the serial killer, not Robert. She'll have to speak to me then . . . to apologize and beg my forgiveness on her knees.*

167

The bus ambled along the busy city streets, heading in the direction of Pembroke Green, Robert's family's city home. Jessica had a date to meet Portia there to try Portia's still-secret scheme for getting Lady Pembroke to talk to her. Jessica gazed thoughtfully out the window. As the brick townhouses got fancier, the fences in front of them grew higher. *They're like fortresses—except they're missing moats. How does ol' Porsh expect to storm the gates of Pembroke Green?*

As she hopped off the bus half a block from Pembroke Green, Jessica spotted Portia waiting for her on the· corner and saw the light immediately. Because Portia wasn't alone. Standing at her side was a tall, distinguished man with penetrating hawk-like eyes and a sweep of silver-streaked hair. Walking toward them, Jessica felt her knees weaken. The handsome man was larger than life; he exuded charisma. *Stage presence . . . and sex appeal,* Jessica thought. *Lady Pembroke will be putty in his hands!* But then, who wouldn't be putty in the hands of the finest and most famous Shakespearean actor in the world, Sir Montford Albert?

"Dad, you remember Jessica," said Portia.

Jessica shook Sir Montford's hand, a bedazzled smile on her face. "We met backstage at Portia's play."

"That's right," Sir Montford boomed. "Yes, Portia speaks often about you—I appreciate what a good, supportive friend you've been to her."

"Oh, well, I . . ." Jessica stuttered.

Taking Jessica's arm, Portia steered her toward Pembroke Green. "You see, when you and I were talking yesterday about how difficult Lady Pembroke was being, I suddenly remembered that she's a huge fan of Dad's. And there it was, the solution to your dilemma! You want Lady Pembroke to open the door to you, I guarantee she'll open the door to you . . . when Dad rings the bell."

"It's a stroke of genius," Jessica declared.

"Isn't it? And Dad's such a good sport." Portia blew a kiss to her father. "He just happened to be in town, and I promised it would only take five minutes of his time. It's all turning out as easy as pie!" she chirped cheerfully.

"The door's not open yet," Jessica reminded her.

"Oh, it will be," Portia said with utter confidence. "It will be."

The three strolled up the walk to Pembroke Green and Sir Montford pressed the bell. The butler answered, easing the door open a crack. "May I help you?" he asked in a clipped, discouraging manner.

"Please tell Lady Pembroke that Sir Montford Albert begs a minute of her time," the actor commanded.

The butler's jaw dropped to his chest. Taking advantage of this momentary lapse, Sir Montford stepped into the front hall, Portia and Jessica scooting in at his heels.

"As a matter of fact, she's—but I'm sure—just one—thank you, sir." The butler bowed. "I'll deliver the message."

The butler hurried off. A minute later, Lady Pembroke herself appeared. At the sight of Sir Montford, her blue eyes grew so big, Jessica thought they were going to pop out of her head. She took a step toward them, wobbling slightly. *For heaven's sake,* Jessica thought, astonished. *She's going to faint. Cold-as-ice, hard-as-a-diamond Lady Pembroke is* swooning!

"Oh, my," Lady Pembroke gasped, the handkerchief she clutched in one hand dancing up to her throat and then her lips. "I'm not receiving visitors—my husband is ill . . . but Sir Montford, do come in. Do come in!"

"I won't take but a minute of your time," he began.

"No, no, you must stay for tea," Lady Pembroke begged. "Have a seat . . . please make yourself at home . . . oh, my!"

Portia met Jessica's eye and grinned triumphantly. "We're in!" she whispered.

The handkerchief still fluttering, Lady Pembroke led them to the large, airy drawing room where Jessica had interviewed her a few weeks ago about her missing mink coat. When she and Sir Montford were seated side by side on a plush, brocade-covered sofa, Lady Pembroke seemed to notice Jessica and Portia for the first

170

time. She narrowed her eyes, two spots of angry color rising in her pale, powdered cheeks. "Why, it's you!" she said to Jessica, balling the handkerchief up in her fist. "Who do you think—"

"Ah, you know Jessica," Sir Montford intervened smoothly. "My dear daughter Portia's friend. How delightful."

Lady Pembroke bit back any further nasty remark she was about to make. "Delightful—yes, it certainly is," she simpered. "But Sir Montford!" Lady Pembroke batted her eyelashes. "To what do I owe the honor—the profound honor—of this visit?"

"I come as a humble petitioner on behalf of my new Edinburgh Theater Company," Sir Montford explained, his voice warm and melodious. "As you know, it requires quite an investment to launch a new theatrical enterprise. Hence, in my capacity as director, I am approaching those very special people—a small group of deeply dedicated, highly cultured friends of the arts—whom I imagine, whom I fondly hope, will be persuaded to serve as patrons of the company. I count you, Lady Pembroke, among that number."

Lady Pembroke touched the diamond necklace encircling her throat. "You do?"

"But of course," Sir Montford said gallantly, accepting a cup from a maid who had just rolled in a teacart laden with china and silver. "There is no more devoted lover of the theater in all of London than Lady Henrietta Pembroke." He winked at Portia. "It's common knowledge."

"I try to do my part," Lady Pembroke said modestly. "And nothing would make me happier than to help further your efforts in Edinburgh. Please put me down for . . ."

She murmured an enormous monetary amount. Sir Montford clasped her bejeweled hand, raising it to his lips. "You are so generous. I cannot thank you enough."

"Oh, well, my . . ."

While Lady Pembroke blushed and babbled, Sir Montford shot a glance at his daughter. Portia nodded.

Releasing Lady Pembroke's hand, Sir Montford rose to his feet. "Thank you for your pledge, and for your hospitality, Lady Pembroke," he said. "And please extend my best wishes to Lord Pembroke for a speedy recovery."

"So soon? Well, this was—oh—good-bye!"

With a crisp bow, Sir Montford disappeared into the hallway. Lady Pembroke watched him until he was out of sight. Turning back, she saw the two girls still sitting in matching velvet wing chairs and jumped.

The expression that had softened for Sir Montford once again became cold and unyielding. Pointedly remaining standing, Lady Pembroke waited in hostile silence for Jessica and Portia to make their exits as well.

Calmly, Jessica lifted her teacup to her lips. "These cakes are delicious," she said, her eyes meanwhile adding, *and I'm not going anywhere, so don't bother glaring at me like that.*

Lady Pembroke sat down stiffly. *This is it,* Jessica thought, her throat suddenly dry. *This is my chance, the only one I'm going to get. I can't blow it. I can't let Robert down.*

Jessica looked at Portia for support and then put down her teacup. *Don't beat around the bush—don't give her time to make up any lies.* Staring straight at Lady Pembroke, Jessica aimed right for the bull's-eye. "I know about Annabelle," she bluffed. "Your husband told me everything."

Lady Pembroke had been leaning forward to spoon sugar into her tea. At Jessica's surprising declaration, she dropped the spoon into the cup, splashing tea onto the marble-topped coffee table.

It worked! Jessica thought. *I caught her off guard. She can't hide it—it's written all over her. She knows about Annabelle, too!*

Taking a damask napkin from the cart, Lady Pembroke dabbed at the spilled tea. Jessica and Portia held their breath.

When Lady Pembroke looked back up at Jessica, the surprise in her eyes had been replaced by a bitter, scornful glint. "Annabelle." Lady Pembroke spat out the name. "Then I suppose you know about the wretched boy."

The boy . . . Robert's brother. "Yes," said Jessica.

173

"Bad enough that Bobby was so tasteless as to be unfaithful with a low-class commoner. He could have walked away from his mistake—should have walked away. Instead, he seemed to feel somehow responsible," Lady Pembroke complained bitterly. "He was constantly throwing our money away on that urchin, but he could never do enough in her opinion. She always wanted more. It went on for years and years."

Lady Pembroke paused just long enough to catch her breath. "And of course, everything he gave to his misbegotten brat was something taken away from our own dear Robert. Why, Bobby even took away little Robert's nanny when Annabelle was sick with pneumonia! It wasn't enough that he had Cameron Neville making house calls every single day. Annabelle needed help, Bobby claimed— his bastard son needed Nanny Millie more than our sweet, pure Robert did."

Sick with pneumonia . . . house calls from Cameron Neville, Jessica thought, her heart racing with excitement. There was one answer already. *Then Lord Pembroke's Annabelle is Dr. Neville's Annabelle S.! And Nanny Millie knew her and the boy. Nanny Millie, who was one of the werewolf's victims!*

Silently, Jessica prayed that Lady Pembroke would keep talking. Appearing to have forgotten that the two girls were even there, Lady Pembroke ranted on to herself, venting the rage of years.

"Of course, everything he did for her had to be

hush-hush so her blind fool of a cuckolded husband wouldn't know that nasty child wasn't his own spawn," Lady Pembroke remembered. "Annabelle and Bobby agreed that she would pretend the money came from the *Journal*, her pension."

Jessica couldn't contain a gasp of surprise. "The *Journal*?"

"She'd worked there—that's how they met. Oh, she was a clever little thing, but it was her undoing. She should have been content with her lot in life instead of trying to steal what wasn't rightfully hers. The nanny incident was the last straw. It was the least he could do for them, Bobby said, but I said anything was too much." A malicious smile curved Lady Pembroke's thin, bloodless lips. "I cut him off. The money is mine, you know," she told her wide-eyed audience. "Bobby didn't bring a farthing into this marriage. Yes, I cut him off," she repeated, gloating and triumphant, "and I got Nanny Millie back. And when Annabelle finally died, I made Bobby swear never to lift a finger for that boy again."

The story of adultery, jealousy, and cruelty raised goose bumps on Jessica's skin. She felt chilled to the bone . . . but also electrified. *It's there, somewhere,* she thought, her head spinning as she struggled to untangle the narrative threads. *The nanny, killed by the werewolf, who isn't Robert so . . . who? Wait. Yes,* Jessica thought. *Yes, it could be . . .*

"The other son," she heard Portia whisper.

Jessica nodded. Of course! The other son, despised and rejected, denied his true father's name, left motherless, penniless . . . *Does the other son know this story?* Jessica wondered. *Could Lord Pembroke's illegitimate son, Robert's mysterious half brother, be the killer?*

Jessica opened her mouth to ask the burning, urgent question: Who is he and where is he now?

But Lady Pembroke spoke first. "Besides, I knew that boy was no good," she concluded. "I knew just from his name. Lucas is an evil name."

Lucas. The blood drained from Jessica's face, leaving her as white as the curtain that fluttered at the window, as white as the sheets that had been on her bed at Pembroke Manor. The sheets that she and Elizabeth and Luke saw soaked with Joy Singleton's blood that Saturday at dawn. Luke . . .

Luke, whose mother had worked for the *Journal* and died when he was a child. Luke, who was obsessed with werewolves . . .

Who would have a better motive? Jessica's heart leapt to her throat, choking her. "Luke Shepherd is Annabelle's son," she cried hoarsely. "Luke is the killer!"

Chapter 11

Without further explanation, Jessica sprang to her feet and bolted out of the drawing room and down the hallway, Portia sprinting after her.

"Jessica, wait!" Portia panted. "Have you gone crazy? What are you talking about? You can't mean Luke Shepherd, Liz's boyfriend from work, is—"

"That's exactly what I do mean," declared Jessica, brushing past the Pembrokes' startled butler and shoving open the heavy front door. "It all adds up, Porsh! Annabelle S., remember? S. is for Shepherd! It threw me off when Elizabeth said Luke's mother's name was Ann, but obviously Ann is just short for Annabelle. Or maybe Annabelle was Lord Pembroke's own private name for her. Whatever, it's the same woman, so Luke is Lord Pembroke's illegitimate son!"

"Wow," said Portia as they clattered onto the sidewalk. "So, where are we going now? To the police?"

"We have to go back to HIS first." Jessica waved her arms for a taxi as she jogged along. "We have to make sure Liz is OK and keep her away from Luke. God, why didn't I figure this out sooner? Why did I write Luke off as harmless?"

Spotting a red telephone booth, Jessica skidded to a stop. "I'm going to call the dorm," she told Portia. "We can't waste a minute. For all we know, she's getting ready for a date with Luke right now!"

Her hand was shaking so much, she could hardly insert the coins into the phone, and then her fingers felt so fat and clumsy, dialing the HIS hall phone number was almost impossible. And then it rang and rang and rang . . .

Pick up, somebody! Jessica thought desperately.

"Hello?" a voice said at last.

"David, is that you?" Jessica cried. "It's me, Jessica. I need to speak to my sister—it's a matter of life and death!"

"Hold on, I'll fetch her," David offered.

He seemed to be gone for an hour. Jessica stared through the glass panes of the phone booth, her brain fizzing with horrible images. Luke creeping into her bedroom at Pembroke Manor in Robert's silk bathrobe . . . returning to take care of the cook . . . going after the poor old nanny . . . attacking his own father. *And Elizabeth trusts him. Elizabeth loves him!*

"Jessica, are you still there?"

"Yes, yes!" she shouted. "Where is Elizabeth?"

"I don't know," said David. "Not here, anyway. I checked your room, and the dining room, and the library. Maybe she's working late."

"Working late," Jessica muttered. Hanging up on David, she stuck in another coin and dialed the *Journal*.

"No," said the receptionist, "she's not here. She left a while ago, with Tony."

Tony! Jessica's knees buckled with relief. *Of course, she's with Tony.* They probably had gone off to look into a story together, or maybe they'd just stopped for a cup of tea. They could be anywhere in London—that thought was somewhat distressing. But at least they were together.

"One more phone call," Jessica signaled to Portia. She might as well ring up Tony's home number. If nothing else, she could leave a message. It was time to start spreading the word about the danger, and she'd need Tony's advice about what to do next.

To her surprise, Tony himself answered the phone. "Hullo?" He sniffled.

"Tony, it's Jessica. Is Elizabeth there?"

She had to hold the phone away from her ear as Tony sneezed loudly on the other end. "Elizabeth? No, why do you ask?"

Jessica's heart dropped into her shoes. In an instant, her feelings of relief and security vanished like smoke, dread and uncertainty taking their

179

place. "Where is she? Do you know?"

She heard Tony blow his nose. "She's doing some after-hours sleuthing. She went over to Annabelle's."

"Annabelle's?" Jessica gasped. "How did she find out about—but Annabelle is dead!"

"I know, but we found her address among Lord Pembroke's, um, papers. She's dead and buried, but Liz thinks there might be a connection between the story of the love affair and the murders. She's hoping to find some clues at Annabelle's old address that will lead her to . . . Excuse me, Jess—I know it hurts your feelings, but I must say it: to Robert."

No, Jessica thought. *It won't lead her to Robert . . . but it very well might lead her straight to the werewolf's lair!* "She went alone?"

"We'd planned to go together, but I'm feeling a bit under the weather." Tony sneezed as if to illustrate the point. "I insisted she take someone with her, though, as protection. The killer could strike again at any moment, and if it turns out that there is something important to be found at Annabelle's, that could make it a dangerous place. She said she'd ask . . ."

No, Jessica thought, knowing who Tony would name even before he said the word. *No. Anyone but . . .*

" . . . Luke."

"The address," Jessica choked out, her heart

180

freezing into a ball of ice in her chest. "Do you remember the address?"

"Well, let's see. I don't quite—not the exact number, no," said Tony, befuddled. "It's on Forget-Me-Not Lane somewhere. But, Jessica, why—"

Dropping the phone, Jessica exploded out of the booth. Eyes wide and hair flying, she ran out into the street, waving her arms madly. "Taxi!" she shouted. "Taxi!"

"Are you familiar with this part of London?" Elizabeth asked Luke as their cab whisked them through a residential area east of downtown.

Luke stared out the window at the city, gray and dusky in the twilight. "Yes, somewhat," he replied. "I know someone who lives around here."

"Who knows what we'll find at Annabelle's old address." Elizabeth pulled out her notebook and thumbed through it, pausing to skim the notes she'd scribbled after the previous day's visit to Pembroke Manor. "If nothing else, I guess I'm just curious to see where she lived." She looked at Luke, her eyes glowing. "Don't you wonder what she was like?"

Luke nodded without speaking, his own eyes dark and unreadable.

"I bet she was beautiful," Elizabeth mused. "Annabelle is a beautiful name, don't you think? There was something very special about her, anyway. But I think it's so sad that she and Lord

Pembroke couldn't love each other openly, couldn't lead a normal life."

Elizabeth tapped the page where she'd copied down a few lines from Annabelle's last letter to Lord Pembroke. "I wonder if they were still seeing each other at this point, or if they'd ended the affair. Lina said there was a scandal in the family, but eventually it must have blown over—she wasn't even able to remember what it was about. Do you think the scandal affected Annabelle's life?"

"Inevitably," Luke murmured.

"Inevitably . . . yes, of course, you're right," said Elizabeth. "Tony said her husband probably found out about it and left her. She probably had to take care of herself and the child." She shook her head. "That's the really sad part, if you ask me. All last night I lay awake wondering what happened to that poor little boy after his mother died."

Elizabeth bit her lip, wanting to curse herself for her tactlessness. *Duh, no wonder Luke's acting so quiet and withdrawn*, she thought. *Talking like this must remind him of his own mother dying.* Reaching across the wide backseat, she took his hand and squeezed it gently.

The last streaks of red and orange had faded from the western sky when the taxi turned onto Forget-Me-Not Lane, a quiet cul-de-sac in a modest neighborhood on the outskirts of town. Stepping out of the cab, Elizabeth and Luke stood side by side on the walk, gazing at number four, a small house in need of a new coat of paint, but with a well-tended little yard. "It's dark," observed Elizabeth. "No one's home." She pointed to the house next door. "How about talking to the neighbors? We could find out who lives here now—the neighbors might even remember back to the days of Annabelle."

Still staring at the dark house, Luke rocked back on his heels, his hands pushed deep in his trouser pockets. "Let's just try the door," he suggested. "If it's unlocked, we could take a quick look around."

Elizabeth hesitated, but only for an instant. They were so close to solving the mystery. . . . What if Annabelle's husband still lived there, and maybe even her child? It was a possibility. Just think of the clues she and Luke might find!

Breaking into someone's house was against the law, but under the circumstances it was also irresistibly tempting. "A really quick look," Elizabeth said as they strode up the walk. "I don't want to get caught."

On the front step, they looked around to make sure none of the neighbors were watching. The streets and sidewalks were empty, except for a homeless man about half a block away, pushing a grocery cart piled high with junk.

Luke put his hand on the doorknob. "Are you ready?" he asked, his voice low and vibrant.

Elizabeth nodded, a rush of adrenaline flooding her veins.

She held her breath as Luke turned the knob and gave a slight push. The door swung inward.

Tentatively, they stepped into the dark entryway. Elizabeth felt around on the wall for a light switch. She located one, but when she flicked the switch upward, the hall remained dark. "The light's not working," she told Luke.

He disappeared into the first room opening off the hallway. "No lights in there, either," he reported, returning a moment later. "The power must be out."

"Shoot," said Elizabeth. "Why didn't I bring a flashlight?"

They stood for a moment in the shadows. "We could leave," Luke said softly.

She couldn't read his expression in the darkness. "No," Elizabeth replied. "We're here. Let's go for it."

Crossing the dark hallway, Luke fumbled with the drawer of a table that was pushed up against the wall. Two empty brass candlesticks stood on top. "Candles," he declared, holding one up. "And matches."

"Then we're all set!"

There was a dry, raspy sound as Luke struck a match. Light flared. Lighting the candles, Luke handed one to Elizabeth. Then, taking the other, he nodded toward a door under the stairs. "I bet that's the basement," he said. "Why don't I check down there for a fuse box? Maybe I can get the power back on."

"I'll wait here," said Elizabeth, not terribly eager to explore the house by herself.

Luke disappeared through the door to the basement. Elizabeth listened to his footsteps creaking down the stairs. Then there was silence.

The candle flame flickered, wavering in the cool draft that had crept up from the basement. Elizabeth pressed her back against the wall, glancing around nervously. *What's taking him so long?* she wondered, even though she knew Luke had only been gone a minute or so.

The house was perfectly still and dark and quiet. Even so, it felt alive to Elizabeth—it seemed to breathe and pulse with ghosts. "Annabelle lived here," she whispered to herself. "She sat in one of these rooms and wrote letters to Lord Pembroke. She nursed their baby here. She died here."

What secrets were hidden in this haunted house?

A shiver shook Elizabeth's body from head to toe. Stepping forward, she paced down the hall. It definitely felt better to move around; it was too creepy just standing there waiting. *Besides, I don't want to be hanging out right there in case somebody comes in. . . .*

At the bottom of the staircase to the second floor, she paused, peering up into the darkness. Then, her candle held bravely out in front of her, she put her foot on the first step.

°   °   °

185

"Jessica? Jessica, are you there?" When there was no response, Tony replaced the telephone receiver, his brow furrowed. "Now, that was odd," he murmured. "Or maybe my head's just fuzzy from this cold. No . . ." He was contagious, maybe, but not delirious. "Something's wrong—something's very wrong."

Picking up the phone again, he dialed Lucy's home number. "Frank, what do you want?" she asked suspiciously when he identified himself.

"Don't worry, I'm not calling to ask you to go out with me," he said dryly. *Not that I wouldn't if I thought for a second that you'd say yes.* "I got your message about keeping work and personal life separate. But listen to this. . . ."

Quickly, he recounted his brief conversation with Jessica, filling Lucy in on the Annabelle angle at the same time. "Something's amiss," he concluded, sneezing. "Last I heard, Jessica wasn't speaking to Elizabeth. Now she's worried to death about her."

"To death. God, Frank, you don't think it has anything to do with . . ."

"With the murders? With Robert?" Tony said grimly. "It very well might. Liz may be in trouble—both girls may be in trouble. What do you say I come get you and we go to Annabelle's after them?"

He half expected Lucy to blow him off, to suspect that he was just trying to finagle a date, but

186

she didn't hesitate. "We must," she agreed. "This sounds serious, Frank—you sound serious. And you're right, they're our interns. We have a responsibility to protect them."

"And to get the story," Tony added. "This could be it, Lucy."

"I'll be waiting for you on the curb," she said, ringing off.

Elizabeth walked slowly up the stairs, one hand shielding the candle flame. At the top of the stairs, she paused, listening to the silence. The dancing flame caused eerie shadows to flicker on the walls, shapes that seemed both to beckon her and to warn her back.

A doorway yawned, dark and intriguing. Elizabeth stepped through it, the candle held high to light her way.

The room was large but sparsely decorated, with only three pieces of furniture: a four-poster bed, matching antique dresser, and night table. The master bedroom, Elizabeth surmised.

The room was strangely bare of ornament: no pictures on the wall, no shoes on the floor, no clutter. It was a man's room, she decided after peeking into the walk-in closet and seeing no sign of a woman's clothing or toiletries.

Elizabeth wandered over to the dresser. Only two things rested on top of the recently dusted surface: an old-fashioned man's shaving brush in a

187

china cup and a photograph in a silver frame.

Elizabeth lifted the photograph to look at it by the warm flickering light of the candle. It was a portrait of an exquisitely beautiful raven-haired woman holding a toddler with ringlets as dark as her own. The woman's smile was reminiscent of Mona Lisa's; her lips curved, but her eyes remained somehow shuttered and mysterious.

Studying the picture, Elizabeth's heart skipped a beat. Something about the woman's face was familiar. *Or is it the baby's face?* Elizabeth wondered. *Where have I seen these people before?*

Tucking the picture frame under her arm, she padded back out into the hallway. There were two other doors. The first turned out to be the bathroom. The second was another bedroom.

She pushed the bedroom door open, the candlelight preceding her into the room. Immediately, she was struck by the very different appearance of this bedroom. *It looks lived in,* she thought, taking another step forward. There were shelves overflowing with books and a desk cluttered with odds and ends. The walls were papered with photos and newspaper clippings—the whole room was like one big bulletin board.

A kid's room, Elizabeth thought, holding out the candle so she could get a better look at the stories tacked up on the wall. *A teenager—maybe someone my age. Someone with a lot of hobbies and interests!*

Curious, she held the candle closer in order to read one of the yellowed newspaper articles. The name in the headline jumped out at her, hitting her like a splash of cold water in the face. Pembroke.

"What's this?" Elizabeth said out loud. The candle nearly went out as she spun around to examine the other clippings. There was another and another and another about the Pembrokes, ranging from social-page items nearly a decade old to the latest newspaper coverage of Robert Junior being sought as a suspect in the werewolf killings.

No, Elizabeth thought, her blood slowly turning to ice in her veins. *They can't all be.* But they were. Every single clipping related to the Pembrokes.

Her teeth chattering, Elizabeth turned on her heel to survey each of the four walls in turn. "Who lives here?" she whispered to herself. "Who lives in Annabelle's old house?" It must have been someone who had known Annabelle . . . and who knew about Annabelle's connection to the Pembroke family. It was too coincidental otherwise. Was it Annabelle's son, all grown up?

At the desk, Elizabeth put down the candlestick and the silver-framed photograph. Picking up a red spiral notebook, she opened to a page at random. *It's a diary,* she realized. *I shouldn't read it. I'd hate it if a stranger read my journal. But . . .*

She couldn't tear her eyes from the page. Holding the notebook so that the candlelight fell on it, she read the first sentence. "I woke up again in a strange place, in the woods outside my father's country home." The script was slanted and dark, as if the person had scrawled the words quickly, pressing down hard with the pen. Elizabeth felt a shock of recognition. *I've seen this handwriting before . . . but where?*

She read on. "I don't know how I got there—I have no memory of journeying from London. My clothes were filthy and ripped and there were drops of blood spattered on my shirt . . . my own blood or someone else's? Did I try to prevent a crime . . . or did I commit one?"

Elizabeth dropped the notebook, her mouth suddenly dry with fear. She stared up at the werewolf clippings on the wall. *Who lives here?*

Behind her, she heard a creak . . . the door easing open. She whirled around, just as a muffled voice asked, "Do you like my collection?"

A scream of terror exploded from Elizabeth's throat, shattering the shadowy stillness of the house.

The werewolf crouched in the doorway. His eyes were red in the dim light and his fangs glistened; the flickering candle cast a huge, hairy, monstrous shadow on the wall behind him. Elizabeth screamed again.

At last, she had found the werewolf . . . or, rather, he had found her.

Chapter 12

Elizabeth stared at the wolfman, her heart pounding wildly. Each second that she waited for him to roar and leap forward to attack her seemed to last an eternity. *I'm going to die,* she thought, vivid memories of the recent tragedies flashing through her panicked brain. *With my throat ripped out, ravaged, in a pool of crimson blood, like Dr. Neville and Joy and Mildred Price. . . .*

She clutched the desk behind her, her eyes darting around the room in search of a way to escape. The werewolf, meanwhile, didn't move.

As Elizabeth looked at him again, suddenly wondering if she were dreaming, if the ominous figure were just a figment of her imagination, she noticed something for the first time. The creature was wearing gray flannel trousers and a navy sweater over an Oxford shirt. *Ohmigod, it's not the werewolf at all. It's Luke!* she realized, her knees buckling with relief.

"Luke!" Elizabeth gasped, laughing at how fooled and frightened she'd been by the lifelike mask. "Oh, Luke, you scared me to death. Take that thing off and help me figure out what we've found here."

"I can't take it off, Elizabeth," Luke said hoarsely. "I can't take it off. Don't you see?"

He took a step toward her, his posture menacing. As he lifted his hands, Elizabeth saw that his fingers were clenched into claws; the muscles in his broad shoulders were bunched and tense. Through the holes in the mask, his eyes glittered at her—glittered with rage and hunger and despair. "I can't," Luke repeated, his voice a husky growl. "It's not a mask."

Do you like my collection? Don't you see?

In a lightning flash of illumination, Elizabeth did see . . . at long last, and all too clearly. "This is your room," she whispered. She shot a glance at the photograph resting on the desk. *Of course— she looks familiar because Luke showed me a picture of his mother the very first day we met.*

The picture was of Luke and his mother . . . Annabelle. Luke was Annabelle and Lord Pembroke's son.

And Luke, Elizabeth's dear friend . . . her love . . . was a madman. Luke was the werewolf of London.

❊   ❊   ❊

Raindrops splattered on the windshield of Tony's car as he and Lucy sped through town toward Forget-Me-Not Lane. "I'll never forgive myself if anything happens to Luke or the girls," he muttered, flicking on the windshield wipers. The light at the intersection ahead turned red and he slammed on the brakes, cursing under his breath at the delay. "Why did I encourage Liz to stick out her neck like this, playing detective? She's just a summer intern, an amateur. I should have left her on Bumpo's beat where she'd be safe."

I didn't think this man ever took anything seriously, Lucy thought, touched. *But he's really worried—he really cares.* "Elizabeth may be young, but she's a journalist," Lucy consoled him. "Remember how she and her sister snuck over to the scene of the Neville murder behind my back? She follows her instincts—she follows the story. I don't think there's anything you could have done to stop her."

Tony raked a hand through his rumpled hair. "Still . . ."

"Still," Lucy agreed with an anxious sigh.

The light changed to green, and Tony stepped on the gas, tires squealing. Lucy studied his profile, a sudden and surprising feeling of warmth flooding through her. "You know, Frank," she said, "I think this is the first time we've ever seen eye-to-eye on anything."

He glanced at her, an ironic smile lifting one

corner of his mouth. "We must be getting soft in our dotage, Friday. We're like two old mother hens fussing about their chicks."

"I had been thinking about asking for your cooperation," she admitted, "to team up to get the girls to reconcile their differences."

Tony nodded. "It's crazy, don't you think, two sisters being so mad at each other for no good reason?"

"When underneath, they love each other more than anything," said Lucy. "I've never seen such stubbornness!"

"Sometimes the emotional wires get crossed," Tony reflected. "Two people think they can't stand each other, when, in fact, it's just the opposite. They put on a big act, pouring all their energy into a silly feud, but the whole time they really want to . . ."

His voice trailed off and a flush rose in his cheek. Lucy felt her own face grow hot. "Frank, are we still talking about Jessica and Elizabeth?"

Tony cleared his throat. "I thought we were, but . . ." They got stuck at another red light, but this time, Tony didn't seem to mind as much. He turned in his seat, fixing hopeful eyes on Lucy's expectant face. "The Wakefield twins aren't the only ones who've been holding each other at arm's length, are they?"

"No," Lucy said softly.

She took a deep breath and then, reaching across the space that separated them, she placed a hand on Tony's arm. Shyly, Tony covered her hand with his own. "I think the girls are going to work things out," he predicted. "How about us?"

Lucy smiled. "Let's tackle this late-breaking news story head-on—tell it like it is."

"It's our duty as investigative reporters, after all," Tony concurred. "All right—Friday. I mean, boss. I'm madly in love with you and I have been for months."

Bending over, Lucy pressed her lips against Tony's flushed cheek. "Me, too," she whispered.

The light turned green and the car shot forward into the rainy night.

"Can't you go any faster?" Jessica shouted desperately.

The driver met her eye in the rearview mirror and raised an eyebrow, scowling. Portia put a restraining hand on Jessica's arm. "He's already breaking the speed limit," she pointed out. "It would be foolish to risk an accident. We'll be there in a minute or two."

"But what if it's too late?" All traces of Jessica's anger at her sister for accusing Robert had disappeared. Tears streamed down her face. "Liz doesn't know—she doesn't even suspect! She gave the pendant to me, when really all the time she was the one dating a werewolf. She trusts Luke completely, she's totally at his mercy. What if he hurts her? What if . . ."

Jessica buried her face in her hands, tormented

by visions of Luke attacking her sister . . . of Elizabeth's lifeless body, the blood draining away . . .

Portia wrapped her arms around Jessica in a comforting hug. "Maybe Luke is the werewolf, but that doesn't mean he'd harm Elizabeth. They're friends—he loves her."

Jessica shook her head. "It doesn't matter. He's killed so many people, in such a cruel and horrible way. Do you really think he's capable of feeling compassion, or love?"

Portia was silent. The cab hurtled onward, city lights rushing past its windows in a rainy blur.

Jessica gripped the armrest so tightly her knuckles turned white. "It's all my fault," she said, choking back a sob. "If we weren't having this stupid fight, we would have been talking about the case, solving it together. Liz would have been with me at Pembroke Green to hear about Annabelle and Luke."

"Ssh," said Portia. "It's not your fault."

"It is," Jessica insisted. "I shouldn't have been so stubborn. I should have accepted that she was only trying to protect me. If anything happens to her . . ." The tears started to flow again. "I won't be able to go on living."

Portia patted Jessica's hand. Since there was no use yelling at the cabbie, Jessica squeezed her eyes shut and prayed. *Please, let me get there in time,* she chanted silently, rubbing Annabelle's silver pendant like a talisman. *Please, let me get there in time. . . .*

Still wearing the werewolf mask, Luke took another step toward Elizabeth. Edging around the desk, she flattened herself against the wall. "Luke, no," she whispered, terror robbing her of her voice.

As if in response to her plea, Luke froze in his tracks. Then Elizabeth saw that he was looking not at her, but at the framed photograph she'd carried from the other bedroom.

"My mother," Luke said, his rough voice softening. He lifted the picture and gazed at it reverently. "Ann . . . Annabelle. That's what my father—my real father—called her. He ruined her life, you know, the high and mighty Lord Pembroke. Abandoned her, abandoned both of us. Me, his own flesh and blood. Then, when she got sick, he let her die." Luke's voice cracked with remembered pain. "My other father, too—her husband. That quack doctor, Neville, and Nurse Handley. They all just let her die. They thought she was bad, but they were the bad ones. She was good—too good for this world. . . ."

Elizabeth stared at Luke, her breath coming fast. Luke had gone over the edge; he appeared to be in a sort of trance. The boy she knew . . . the boy she loved . . . would never hurt her, but this was someone else. Luke's animal side, his dark side had taken over, and it was far darker than Elizabeth ever could have guessed.

197

If I could only get the other Luke back, she thought desperately. *But how?* "Yes," she whispered, praying she would be able to keep the werewolf gentle. "She was too good."

His anger flaring again, Luke slammed the picture frame on the desk. Elizabeth jumped. "Can you imagine how I felt, that weekend at Pembroke Manor?" he snarled. "Seeing everything that should have been my mother's . . . that should have been mine. And your stupid sister, practically licking young Lord Robert's boots, and looking down her nose at me. Who did she think she was? Did she think she was going to be Lady Pembroke someday, when my own mother had been denied that privilege?"

Elizabeth licked her lips, which were as dry as paper. She was looking at the person who had stalked to Jessica's bedroom with murder on his mind . . . only to kill the wrong sleeping blond girl. "I—I—" she stuttered.

Luke cut her off, his hand slashing the air like a blade. "I was only eight years old as I stood by my mother's deathbed," he remembered. "With her last breath, she told me the truth. She told me who I really was. And I knew that someday . . ."

Elizabeth's eyes darted around the room. *There's got to be a way out. Someone has to come. Oh, please, don't let me die here.* "Someday . . . what?" she prompted, trying to keep Luke talking, knowing that her only hope was to stall for time.

"Someday I'd get back at the people who hurt her—the people who denied me. There have been so many." Luke's voice deepened to a hoarse, heartbroken growl. He took another step—he was only a few feet away from her now. "So many," he repeated, raising his arms as if to grasp Elizabeth by the throat. "But someday, I'd get them all."

"Luke, stop," Elizabeth begged, her throat constricting as if she could already feel the grip of sharp claws, the slash of beastly fangs. "Take off the mask. It's me. I can help you."

It was no use. Luke didn't see or hear her; he heard and saw only the demons in his own soul.

Elizabeth closed her eyes, trembling and dizzy with terror. Luke—her death—was almost upon her. She could feel the warmth of his breath . . . something furry brushed her arm. . . .

She waited for the blow to fall—she waited for the werewolf's bloodthirsty howl of triumph.

Instead, from the other side of the room, a strong male voice rang out, shattering the fateful silence. "Stop right there, Luke. Don't move another inch or I'll end it all. I have the silver bullet!"

Elizabeth's eyelids popped open. To her astonishment, the homeless man she'd seen outside with the grocery cart was now standing in the bedroom doorway, a gun raised and pointed straight at Luke's heart. With his grimy cap removed, Elizabeth recognized him instantly. "Robert!" she cried.

At that instant, another young man burst into the room, his face pale and his dark eyes wide. *Rene!* Even more incredible, right on Rene's heels was Sergeant Bumpo of Scotland Yard.

Luke whirled to face his challengers. "Robert, watch out!" Elizabeth screamed.

With an enraged roar, Luke lunged for Robert, grabbing the arm that held the gun. The two toppled to the floor, rolling over and over. Sergeant Bumpo and Rene dove into the fray, trying to seize Luke's arms and pin him, but Luke's madness seemed to give him the strength of ten men—he didn't relinquish his hold on Robert.

He'll kill him, Elizabeth thought, gnawing her fingernails. *Luke is going to kill Robert . . . his own half brother.*

There were groans and curses as the four men continued to scuffle frantically. Elizabeth held her breath, agonized by her helplessness. "Luke, stop," she cried. "Stop before it's too late."

It's over, Elizabeth thought a moment later. Robert appeared to have Luke pinned to the ground. But then, with a superhuman effort, Luke hurled Robert off him and leapt back to his feet. Robert lost his grip on the gun; it clattered to the ground. Elizabeth caught a glimpse of the weapon, but then it disappeared. Someone else had grabbed it . . . but who?

She started forward and then staggered back when a shot rang out. The blast was deafening in the small room. It echoed, penetrating Elizabeth's heart with a sharp knifelike pain as if she herself had been mortally wounded. "Who's been shot?" she cried out.

At the sound of the gunshot, all four men had frozen. Now three of them—Robert, Rene, and Sergeant Bumpo—remained standing. With a startled gasp, Luke toppled backward, a hole in the breast of his sweater where the bullet had torn through.

Rushing forward, Elizabeth knelt at Luke's side. The werewolf mask slipped off and she found herself gazing down at his face. It was the familiar, beloved face of the boy she'd met that first day at the *Journal*. The other Luke, the gentle, kind, poetic Luke, was back.

But not for long. Even though she was half blinded by tears, Elizabeth could see that Luke's fair skin was whiter than ever. His lifeblood was ebbing away, the light in the blue eyes growing dimmer and dimmer.

Clasping his hand in both of hers, Elizabeth willed Luke to hold on to life. But it was no use. "We did it, Elizabeth," Luke whispered, gazing up at her with a beatific smile. His eyelids fluttered and drooped. "We killed the werewolf."

Like a candle being snuffed out, the light in Luke's eyes flickered and died.

In front of the house at number four Forget-Me-Not Lane, Jessica and Portia converged with

Tony and Lucy. Guided by Tony's flashlight, all four dashed inside and up the stairs, following the sounds of shouting.

Halfway up the stairs, they heard the sharp crack of a pistol shot. "No!" Jessica cried. "Oh, God, he's killed her!"

They pounded down the hallway and then stopped at the door to a candelit bedroom, arrested by the somber tableau within.

Looking past Tony's shoulder, Jessica saw her sister bent over Luke Shepherd's motionless body. Rene Glize crouched next to Elizabeth, one hand resting on her shoulder.

Above them stood Sergeant Bumpo, a smoking gun in one hand and a walkie-talkie in the other. And next to the detective . . . Robert, dressed in the rags of a homeless person, gazing down remorsefully at his dead half brother.

The adrenaline that had fueled Jessica's body drained from her veins and she went limp. *It's over*, she realized numbly. *It's all over.*

Chapter 13

As the twins stepped out of the taxi in front of HIS, the first pink blush of dawn was just warming the eastern sky. Jessica stretched her arms over her head, yawning. "Talk about being late for curfew!" she joked tiredly. "Mrs. Bates will have our heads."

After talking all night with the police and Scotland Yard, with Tony and Lucy and Rene, and with her parents long distance, Elizabeth was too exhausted to speak or even smile. Her eyes on the ground, she turned away from the street to trudge slowly toward the dorm.

Before Elizabeth could insert her key in the door, Jessica touched her arm. "Let's not go in just yet," Jessica said softly. "Let's watch the sunrise."

Side by side, they sat down on the stone steps in front of HIS. In silence, they watched as the first faint streaks of pink brightened to orange and overhead the dark sky turned robin's-egg blue. "No fog, for once," observed Jessica. "It's going to be a sunny day."

Elizabeth drew in a deep, bracing breath of fresh morning air, her gaze fixed on the yellow rays of sunlight streaming through the trees in the park. *A new morning, a sunny day. For me and Jessica, maybe, but not for Luke. . . .*

A solitary tear trickled down Elizabeth's cheek. A second later, she felt Jessica pressing something into her hand. "A couple of Tony's tissues," Jessica explained wryly. "He had about ten boxes with him, so I snagged some."

Elizabeth dabbed her eyes and nose. "Thanks," she said, her voice scratchy. "And . . . thanks for forgiving me for all the bad and untrue things I said about Robert."

"You were only judging by the evidence," Jessica said generously. "And it's not like you were the only one. Everyone in London, including the police, saw it the same way."

"Still." Taking another tissue, Elizabeth blew her nose. "I kept accusing you of being blind and infatuated, when the whole time . . ."

"We were both doing the best we could with what we knew," said Jessica.

Elizabeth sighed. "I suppose you're right. It's funny, though, isn't it? We were both working on the Annabelle puzzle, but we didn't know it."

"That's right," said Jessica. "I found the file at Dr. Neville's—"

"And I found the books and love letters in the secret werewolf library."

"We both suspected she was important," said Jessica. "We were right, too."

"If only we could have solved the puzzle sooner." Elizabeth hugged her knees, fighting back another wave of bitter, regretful, pointless tears. "We might have prevented a lot of pain and grief. We might have saved lives. We might have saved . . ."

She didn't speak it, but the name hung in the cool morning air between them. *Luke. We might have saved Luke.*

"We should have been working together," Jessica agreed. "We always work best as a team."

Inching over on the step, Jessica wrapped an arm around her sister's shoulders. They sat that way for a few minutes, waiting for the sun to burst over the tops of the trees. At last it did, flooding the street and the yard with light and warmth.

Slowly, the twins rose to their feet. Jessica's words were still echoing in Elizabeth's head. *We always work best as a team.* "Let's never fight again," Elizabeth whispered to her sister.

Jessica folded Elizabeth in a warm, tight hug. "OK. Or at least," she added, a smile in her voice, "let's always fight on the same side."

❖   ❖   ❖

There wasn't time to nap—Robert was picking her up in less than an hour to go visit his father in the hospital—but after a long, hot shower, Jessica felt wide awake and energized. Pirouetting in front of the mirror, she admired the crispness of her straw-colored linen suit and sage-green blouse. Just putting on clean clothes made a world of difference.

And breakfast, she thought, her mouth watering in anticipation of eggs, sausage, and home-baked scones. *I'm starving!*

When the Pembroke family limousine pulled up in front of HIS, Jessica flew down the walk to meet it, her body and heart feeling as light and free as a bird. The whole city was sparkling and beautiful . . . and safe. *We don't have to be afraid anymore,* she exulted. *The werewolf's reign of terror is over.*

Robert and the chauffeur stepped out of the limousine at the same time. With Clifford beaming his approval, Robert ran to meet her, and Jessica flung herself into his arms.

The limousine sped through town, Robert and Jessica snuggling close in the backseat. Robert ran a fingertip gently down the side of Jessica's face. "I can't believe I'm really touching you," he said, his voice gruff with emotion. "For a while, I thought I might never again be able to."

Jessica smiled, tugging playfully on the lapels of his navy blazer. "And I might not have let you, either, if you were still dressed in the smelly old rags you were wearing last night!"

Robert grinned. "I hadn't washed my hair for a week, either. Seriously, though." His expression grew solemn. "If I learned anything while I was undercover, it's how powerful personal appearances are. When you're dressed in expensive clothes, people are ready to respect you without knowing anything about you—before you even ask, they're bending over backward to be nice. But when you're grubby and ragged, people look right through you, as if you're less than human. You become invisible."

"That was why it was the best disguise," said Jessica. "You didn't have to leave London—you were right there, right under our eyes the whole time, but we didn't even see you."

"You were right under my eyes," Robert corrected her. "That was the whole point."

"Go back to the beginning," Jessica urged. "I got bits and pieces of it from everybody else last night, but I've been dying to hear the whole story from you."

"The beginning . . . all right," said Robert, stroking Jessica's hair. "You remember the last time we spoke, before I had to disappear?"

"We met for breakfast and you wouldn't tell me a thing," Jessica recalled. "I was so upset. And scared," she admitted. "I mean, not scared of you—scared for you."

"I was a bit scared myself," said Robert. "Who wouldn't be, after learning from my father that the police suspected me of being the most heinous serial killer to strike London since Jack the Ripper?"

"Your father didn't believe it, though," said Jessica. "And I didn't believe it."

"But the evidence was damaging," said Robert. "How did threads from my paisley robe get on the door frame to the room where Joy was murdered? No one was going to believe me if I said I hadn't worn the robe all weekend, much less gone to your room that night. And there was the cigarette case with my initials found by Dr. Neville's body."

"Luke was framing you!"

"Whether intentionally or unintentionally, we'll never know," Robert agreed. "Of course, I didn't suspect Luke at the time—I didn't know anything about him and Annabelle. But I knew someone was framing me, and I knew any jury would find me guilty if I didn't come up with real evidence that pointed to the real killer."

"You went to Nanny Millie's, didn't you?" said Jessica.

Robert nodded. "That first night. I needed a place to stay, and I also needed to talk to someone who had faith in me—who could lift my spirits and give me the courage to face the obstacles ahead of me. She was so kind, as always." Tears sparkled in Robert's deep-blue eyes and he clenched his teeth. "That woman never had anything but kindness for anyone. And to think I led that monster to her!"

"I don't think Luke going after her had anything to do with your visit," Jessica consoled him. "Poor Nanny Millie was already on Luke's list of people who'd betrayed him and his mother."

Robert sighed heavily. "Well, the next morning, the newspapers were all blaring the news—I was a werewolf and wanted for murder. Of course, Nanny didn't believe a word of it. She'd have stood staunchly by me if I'd sprouted fangs and hair right there in front of her. I didn't want to involve her, though, so I took off. If I'd known I'd never see her alive again . . . !"

Jessica squeezed his arm. "You couldn't have known, and you couldn't have prevented her death."

"I just didn't realize she was in any danger," said Robert. "I was too busy worrying about you."

"Me?" said Jessica, pleased.

Robert kissed the tip of her nose. "You. Someone—Luke, as it turns out—had tried to kill you at Pembroke Manor. If he tried again, I intended to be there to stop him. Going undercover as a homeless person, I was free to wander the streets any time of the day or night, to watch over you and Elizabeth and also do some sleuthing. My first day prowling around the park, I saw Luke give Elizabeth the silver bullet and decided I had to get hold of it. I was sure that, sooner or later, I'd come face-to-face with the killer, and I needed to be armed. So I went into your dorm room a few days later and took it from Elizabeth's drawer."

"I knew you were there that morning!" Jessica cried. "Oh, I wanted so much to see you!"

"For your own protection, I couldn't let that happen." Robert pressed a kiss on top of her hair. "But it broke my heart to see you crying."

"The silver bullet," Jessica mused, resting her cheek against Robert's broad chest. "Luke—werewolf Luke—must have been the one who tore our room apart later that same day. He must have known the bullet might be used against him."

"It was Luke," Robert confirmed. "When Sergeant Bumpo came back out of the dorm that evening, I pretended to be drunk—stumbling over my own feet and shouting obscenities at him. The poor man had no choice but to cuff me and take me in."

"But why did you do that?" asked Jessica. "You had to know the police were going to find out who you really were, and—"

"That was the point," Robert explained. "I revealed my true identity to Sergeant Bumpo on the way to the station. Was he flabbergasted! He thought that somehow he'd managed to catch the serial killer all by himself."

Jessica was beginning to feel lost in the complexity of Robert's tale. "Wait a minute. You said it was Luke who ransacked our room. How did you know?"

"I saw him enter HIS and then leave again not long before you and Liz came home and discovered the vandalism," he replied. "I told Bumpo, and he agreed Luke warranted watching. He also agreed not to turn me in—he booked me on vagrancy charges and I spent the night in a cell. That was the same night my father was attacked at Pembroke Green."

"So that proved you weren't the werewolf!" Jessica exclaimed.

"Right—it cleared me in Bumpo's mind and he decided I might be onto something. We both started watching Luke." Robert's face darkened. "But not quite closely enough. If it had taken us just a minute longer to get to the house on Forget-Me-Not Lane . . ."

"You got there in time. Thank God, you got there in time." Jessica threw her arms around Robert, her eyes brimming with grateful tears. "You're heroes, both of you. You saved my sister's life."

Robert returned Jessica's embrace. "But my brother lost his life," he said sadly. "My poor half brother. Will we ever understand what was really going on in his troubled, twisted mind?"

Elizabeth sat alone in her dorm room, an afghan wrapped around her legs and a red spiral notebook lying closed on her lap. She knew, at some point, Scotland Yard would want the notebook as evidence, but in the meantime, she needed it herself. She needed to read it, if she could force herself to. She needed to make one final effort to understand who Luke Shepherd really was.

It was the notebook Elizabeth had read from as she stood in Luke's bedroom in the house on Forget-Me-Not Lane. The same notebook that he'd been scribbling in when she surprised him at the *Journal* the day they met. *I caught him writing poetry,* she remembered. *He was so embarrassed.*

Elizabeth drew a deep, shaky breath, bracing herself. With trembling fingers, she opened the notebook.

It did contain poetry, but for the most part the notebook had been used as a journal. The first entries had been made when Luke was nine or ten. He had started writing things down after his mother died, Elizabeth observed. The poor little boy—he was so lonely, so confused!

In simple, childish diction, Luke wrote about missing his mother. Her death, and the secret she'd told him, had thrown his young life into disorder. He was curious about his "real" father, but also distressed. "How can Lord Pembroke be my daddy if I've never met him?" nine-year-old Luke had written. "What about the daddy I live with, who takes care of me? Since I'm not really his, he must not love me—he must only be pretending to love me. I wish that other family would come and take me away. Why don't they? Don't they want me?"

Elizabeth shook her head, her heart aching in sympathy. "He would have been better off not knowing the truth—Annabelle should never have told him," she said aloud. "How different things might have been!"

She turned a blank page and read on. Apparently, Luke had abandoned the diary for a number of years, taking it up again at the age of thirteen.

The tone had changed. Intense, focused bitterness took the place of the earlier childish uncertainty. The pages burned with anger at the biological father who had never acknowledged him, with resentment of the whole Pembroke family, especially the legitimate son and heir, Robert. "That spoiled boy has everything in the world," Luke wrote, underlining "spoiled" with dark strokes. "Today the whole city of London can read in the newspaper that he was expelled from another school. He has so many privileges, so many advantages, so much wealth, that he can afford to just throw it all away. There will always be more. How ashamed his father, our father, must be. If I had the chance, how proud I could make him!"

It was natural for him to be angry, Elizabeth reflected. Maybe even understandable that he would be sort of obsessed by the Pembrokes. But at some point, Luke had crossed over a line. His emotions had grown so warped, they took on a life of their own.

It's almost as if there were two Lukes, Elizabeth thought. One Luke continued to live the life of a normal teenaged boy, doing well in school and getting along superficially with his nominal father, Mr. Shepherd, who seemed never to have suspected that he wasn't Luke's real parent. While the other Luke . . .

At sixteen, Luke experienced his first blackout. As time passed, they became more and more frequent; not a week went by that he didn't wake up one morning in a strange place, with no idea of how he got there, whole blocks of time a blank in his memory. "What's happening to me?" Luke wrote, his script uneven. "Am I losing my mind?"

"Yes," Elizabeth whispered. "Yes, my poor Luke." He had begun the descent . . . into madness.

With tears in her eyes, she read the final portion of the journal, the entries written during the period that the werewolf was terrorizing London. Luke's split personality was starkly evident. "I finally met him, my own brother," Luke wrote about Robert Pembroke. "I set foot in Pembroke Manor—I shook my father's hand. I think he recognized me, my name, anyway, but he didn't acknowledge me. He won't, ever— He discarded me when he discarded my mother. But he will feel differently in the future. He will regret his mistake, when the entire world learns that his namesake is a killer . . . a werewolf!"

He really believed it was Robert, Elizabeth realized, recalling Luke's dying words. *He had no idea he himself was the murderer.*

Luke had realized that something was wrong with him, though; the diary recorded his growing sense of confusion. "I'm forgetting things," he wrote. "When Robert left his silver cigarette case at the office the other day, didn't I slip it into my pocket? I wanted something that belonged to him . . . it was so elegant, so rich. I held it in my hand, I know I did . . . but then, the case turned up next to Neville's corpse. So it must have fallen out of Robert's pocket, not mine. How could I have such a delusion?"

Elizabeth flipped back a page to an entry written at Pembroke Manor. "I snuck into Robert's room, just to see what it was like, just to imagine it was my room, as it should have been. That closet, full of the most elegant clothing! I couldn't resist slipping on the hunter-green paisley robe, just for a moment."

Elizabeth bit her lip until she tasted blood. *No, you took the robe, Luke. You wore it to Jessica's room that night. You wore it while you killed Joy. . . .*

A week later, Luke wrote of his fears for Elizabeth's safety. "I have vowed to protect her," he recorded. "I love her as I've loved no one since . . . But I begin to doubt my ability to keep her from harm. I begin to doubt myself. I am on the trail of the werewolf—I can feel how close we are to each other. I am just one step behind him. . . . But the blackouts trouble me, frighten me. What do they mean? What is my unconscious trying to tell me?"

The last entry was dated Tuesday, just two days earlier. *The day before his death,* Elizabeth thought, her throat tightening with tears.

"I am too exhausted, too feebleminded to work on the newspaper article my editor has told me she wants by the end of the day," Luke confided to the red spiral notebook. "I slept last night, but not a restful sleep—clearly not, since somehow, while in a dream or trancelike state, I found my way to the other side of town. The rain on my face woke me, as I lay in the leaves in a park just a block from Pembroke Green. There was blood on the sleeves and collar of my shirt . . . I let the rain pour down on me until it was washed away.

"This morning," the diary continued, "hearing the news, I see how close I am to my goal—to catching the werewolf. My father, Lord Pembroke, was attacked last night and I must have been there! I must have come upon the scene. Perhaps I touched my father's body, not knowing he still lived, or perhaps I grappled with the werewolf himself and that is how the blood came to stain me. I can not know for certain because I cannot remember. But it must have happened that way . . . mustn't it?"

I should have guessed, Elizabeth thought, her eyes brimming. *I should have seen that something was wrong. How can I say I loved him when I didn't even know him?*

Distractedly, Elizabeth turned the page. She'd thought she'd reached the end of Luke's diary, but now she found herself staring down at a short poem . . . a love sonnet titled, simply, "Elizabeth."

Elizabeth read the poem, her lips moving silently. *I did know Luke,* she realized, touching the lines on the page with her finger. *I knew this Luke. I loved this Luke. And he loved me. This side of Luke fought so hard against the other side . . . but it was a fight he couldn't win.*

The tears spilled forth, wetting her cheeks. She closed the notebook, whispering, "Good-bye, Luke."

The nurse on duty at the hospital gave Jessica and Robert permission to visit Lord Pembroke. "He's still quite weak, quite delicate, though," she cautioned. "He mustn't be agitated or excited."

Taking Jessica's hand, Robert walked purposefully toward his father's hospital room. Jessica could sense his powerful emotions: eagerness, anxiety, hope, fear, love. *He hasn't seen his father since the attack,* Jessica thought, *and the doctors say Lord Pembroke may not live. This may be the last time. . . .*

Hurrying to his father's bedside, Robert fell on his knees. He grasped the older man's hand and pressed his tear-streaked face against it.

Lord Pembroke had been dozing, but at the sight of Robert, his pale face brightened. "My son," he murmured, his voice trembling with emotion. "My son."

Jessica pulled up two chairs and she and Robert sat down. "So, I gather you've heard the news," Robert said to his father.

Lord Pembroke nodded. "I was told of your vindication, and of Luke's death. I don't know which is greater, my joy at the former or my sorrow at the latter."

"Why didn't you tell me?" Robert burst out. "Why didn't you tell me I had a brother?"

"Your mother couldn't bear for Luke to be part of our lives, and after what I'd done to her, I couldn't wrong her further. It was best for everyone, I thought, that there should be no contact. I had never even seen the boy," Lord Pembroke reminisced, "until the day he came to Pembroke Manor with the girls. When he spoke his name, I knew immediately. It was quite a shock. But it never occurred to me that he knew, that Annabelle had told him his true parentage." His watery eyes dimmed and he picked fretfully at the sheet. "I never meant for him to suffer. I tried to take care of them—I tried to protect them both."

"We know," Robert assured him. "We know you did what you thought best, under the circumstances."

"So many lost souls," Lord Pembroke mourned. "Annabelle, and now our son . . . and all the others. And your mother—I made her so unhappy. She never forgave me. I am responsible for all of it." His voice dropped to a tormented whisper. "Annabelle shared my passion for folklore, and we

218

transmitted it to our boy. I am the father of this tragedy, literally and figuratively."

"You mustn't blame yourself," Robert urged, leaning forward. "We have to put the past behind us. You must get better. I—" His voice cracked. "I need you."

Lord Pembroke grasped Robert's hand and Robert squeezed tightly. Jessica could almost see the life-giving strength flow from son to father. "I'll try, son," Lord Pembroke whispered.

"I always miss out on all the action," Emily bemoaned later that afternoon in the dorm dining room. "I can't believe I was working late on a boring BBC documentary about British immigration policy last night while you and Portia were cracking open the biggest murder case in the history of London!"

Jessica shrugged, feigning modesty. "I guess great detective work is half dumb luck—being in the right place at the right time. The other half, of course," she added with a smug smile, "is sheer raw brainpower."

"You wouldn't have wanted to be there," Portia told Emily. "It was horrible, seeing Luke right after he was shot. And poor Elizabeth, having to witness it. I'll never forget it as long as I live."

"That Luke seemed like a nice bloke." David shook his head. "Never would've picked him for a psycho."

219

"You can't tell—that's how they get away with it for so long," said Emily. "They look and act like anybody else—it's just underneath that they're . . . off."

"The good news is, Robert turned up again and he's a hero," said Portia, smiling at Jessica. "Every cloud has a silver lining."

"I'm split in two," Jessica confessed. "I'm deliriously happy because of Robert, but at the same time I'm miserable for Liz. She wouldn't come down to dinner—she's just lying on her bed staring at the wall. Nothing I do or say seems to make her feel any better."

"She just needs time," said Portia. "Time to heal."

"Look," said Emily, nodding toward the entrance to the dining room. "Maybe she's starting to heal a little already."

After forcing herself to get out of bed, Elizabeth had walked downstairs and bumped into Rene outside the HIS dining room. "Elizabeth," he exclaimed, touching her arm. "I've been thinking about you all day at the embassy. You look well."

Elizabeth smiled tiredly. "No, I don't. I haven't slept in thirty-six hours. But thanks, anyway."

"How about some tea," suggested Rene, ushering her into the dining room.

Elizabeth glanced across the room to see Jessica, Emily, Portia, Gabriello, and David smiling encouragingly at her. Her resolve faltered. *I can't deal with them—I'm just not ready.* "I—I'll sit with you for a minute," she told Rene. "Here, this corner table."

Rene poured two cups of hot tea and filled a plate with scones and sandwiches. For a few minutes, they sat eating in silence. He seemed content just to keep her company; he didn't make conversation. Gratitude filled Elizabeth's grieving heart.

"I wanted to thank you, Rene," she said quietly. "For—for being there last night. "I know you were—I know you would have . . ." She choked on the words.

He put a finger to his lips. "Ssh. It's OK. We don't have to talk about it. I only did what any good friend would do."

She shook her head, smiling. "No, you went out of your way for me—way out of your way! When you couldn't talk me into leaving London, you decided to be my personal bodyguard . . . only, you had to do it from a distance because you knew I'd never put up with it otherwise."

Rene grinned. "It was a challenge. You get around, Elizabeth Wakefield!"

"You trailed me and Tony to Pelham that day," she recalled. "You weren't really visiting a friend of your mother's. And I saw you again at Victoria Station. And last night, you came to Forget-Me-Not Lane. It's funny, I kept getting the feeling that someone was following me. I didn't know I had a guardian angel—I thought it was . . . someone bad."

"I couldn't let anything happen to you," Rene

221

said simply. "But now, I don't have to play private eye anymore, and neither do you. We can return to our normal lives."

Elizabeth's lips trembled. "No, I don't think so," she whispered. "It's not that easy."

"I know it won't be easy." Rene squeezed her hand. "But it will happen. Your friends are here, and we'll help."

All day long, Elizabeth had been fighting back tears, struggling to keep from drowning in an ocean of loneliness and despair. Now, suddenly, she felt as if, against all odds, she'd managed to swim back to shore. The dangerous tide tugged at her ankles, but she was breathing the air—she was safe on the sand. *My friends . . . I'm not alone.*

The tears spilled forth, but they were tears of hope as well as sorrow. "Thanks," Elizabeth repeated. "Thanks for being my friend."

Chapter 14

"I never thought I'd see the day," said Zena, one of Jessica and Elizabeth's *Journal* co-workers, as they stood in a receiving line in the leafy courtyard of a fashionable London hotel on Saturday. "I never thought Tony would get Lucy on a date, much less to the altar!"

"Well, I knew they'd get together sooner or later," claimed Jessica. "I mean, it was inevitable. Like a force of nature or something."

"A force of nature, all right—a tornado," Robert interjected with a grin. "Didn't you say they fell in love on one day, and decided to get married the next?"

"Yes," said Jessica with a happy sigh. "Isn't it the most romantic thing you ever heard?"

In Jessica's opinion, Tony and Lucy couldn't have picked a better time to get swept off their feet by passion. It had been such a depressing week; they all needed a really good party to lift their spirits. And what could be more fun than a wedding?

Even Liz is having a good time, Jessica observed, watching out of the corner of her eye as Rene whispered something in Elizabeth's ear that made her smile. *It might take a while, but we're all going to get over this—all of us.*

It was their turn to greet the bride and groom. Lucy looked stunning and composed in a creamy, tea-length silk dress with her luxurious chestnut hair swept up on her head. Tony, in a suit and tie, looked dazed.

As Jessica flung her arms around Lucy, Robert pumped Tony's hand. "Congratulations, old chap. This is just grand!"

"Isn't it?" Tony marveled. "But I have this lurking suspicion that it's a fever-induced hallucination and any minute now I'll wake up and discover Lucy Friday won't give me the time of day."

His bride slipped a slender arm around his waist and planted a kiss on his cheek, causing him to flush profusely. "That's Lucy Friday Frank," she corrected him.

Tony shook his head, smiling at Jessica and Elizabeth. "I'm right, aren't I? This is a dream?"

"If it's a dream," said Lucy, her own eyes shining, "let's just hope it lasts a lifetime."

After filling their plates at the luncheon buffet

set up just inside the French doors in the airy, elegant dining room, the twins, Robert, and Rene scouted around for table seven. "There it is," said Elizabeth, pointing toward a table across the room near the band. "And you'll never guess who's sitting at the next table."

"The detective from Scotland Yard," exclaimed Rene.

"Sergeant Bumpo!" cried Jessica.

All four burst out laughing. "It's really kind of too bad that he's getting credit for solving such a big crime," mused Jessica. "He's just not going to be the same old bumbling Bumpo."

At that moment, in the process of rising to greet two ladies who were sharing his table, Sergeant Bumpo knocked over his chair. The chair crashed into a potted palm, which in turn toppled onto the startled band members.

"On the other hand, some people never change," said Jessica with a giggle. She hooked her arm through her sister's. "C'mon, Liz. Let's go say hi to the hero of Scotland Yard!"

After a number of friends and relatives had given toasts, Tony Frank himself rose to his feet. "We can't tell you how much it means to us that you were all able to be here on this special occasion, especially on such short notice!" A murmur of laughter ran around the room. "Now, I'd like you to raise a glass with me," Tony requested. Lifting his champagne, he turned to gaze adoringly down at Lucy. "And drink a toast to the most beautiful, talented, and intelligent woman in England, who on this day has made me the happiest man on earth. My wife, Lucy."

Elizabeth clinked her water glass against Jessica's. "Can you believe it was less than a week ago that we both wanted to fix Tony and Lucy up," said Jessica, "but because we weren't speaking to each other, we couldn't work together at it?"

Elizabeth laughed. "I guess they didn't wait around for us."

"Although I think we deserve at least some of the credit for getting this romance off the ground," Jessica declared. "Lucy said so herself. It was when they were frantic about us, and rushing to our aid, that it finally hit them that they were nuts about each other."

"Love always finds a way," said Robert, slipping an arm around Jessica's shoulders.

Jessica beamed up at him, her face glowing. "It does, doesn't it?"

Under the table, Rene reached for Elizabeth's hand to give it a supportive squeeze. Elizabeth made an effort to smile. "I'm OK," she whispered, although she wasn't at all sure she was . . . or would be, ever again.

When Tony sat down again, Lucy herself stood to address her guests. "I know it's not traditional for the bride to give a toast," she announced, "but then, I'm not a traditional bride. And this is not a traditional toast. I just wanted to take advantage of being the center of attention to share some good tidings. Robert Pembroke Junior tells us that his father has turned a corner for the better and will be released from hospital soon."

There were smiles and exclamations of relief at every table. Elizabeth felt her heart swell with emotion. Miraculously, one life that Luke had come so close to destroying had been saved.

"Of course, it will be a while before Lord Pembroke is fully recovered," Lucy continued. "Apparently, he is eager to turn some of the family business over to his highly capable son. One change is already official." Lucy flashed a smile at Robert. "As editor-in-chief of the *London Journal*, I'd like to bid a warm welcome to the new owner of the newspaper: Robert Pembroke Junior!"

A hearty cheer went up. Jessica threw her arms around Robert, bursting with pride. Elizabeth clapped along with the others. "You have to admit it now, Liz," Jessica whispered to her when the fuss finally died down. "Your first impression of Robert was way off base."

Elizabeth nodded. She wouldn't deny that Robert had struck her as self-centered and undeserving. But in recent weeks, faced with unjust accusations and mortal danger, he'd shown courage, initiative, and determination. "I've never claimed to be an infallible judge of character," she whispered back, thinking about Luke Shepherd. "I was wrong about Robert, and I'm glad."

As Lucy and Tony cut the wedding cake, the band struck up a lively tune. Elizabeth smiled at the bride and groom, her eyes sparkling with sentimental tears. *I feel as if I've known them forever,* she reflected, accepting the linen handkerchief Rene offered her. *Tony, Lucy, Rene, the rest of the gang from the dorm . . . I guess because we've been through so much together.*

Her glance shifted from the newlyweds to Jessica and Robert, who stood with their arms wrapped around each other, gazing raptly into each other's eyes. Elizabeth hadn't seen her twin sister so radiantly happy in a long, long time. *She really does care for him,* Elizabeth realized. *Poor thing, her heart is going to break a week from now when our internships end and we have to fly back to the States.*

As for my heart . . . Elizabeth felt a pang for the special friend she'd lost. She thought about their lunches at the Slaughtered Lamb, their walks around the city, their lively discussions about literature and history, movies and art. If she closed her eyes, she could see the sparkle in Luke's lake-blue eyes, the shock of dark hair falling over his pale forehead; she could hear his sweet, adorable English voice; she could feel his hand in hers, the warmth of his lips as they kissed. *My heart has already been broken into a million pieces.*

Silently, deep in her being, Elizabeth said good-bye to the troubled soul of the boy she'd fallen in love with in London. *I'll keep the good memories separate from the bad,* she decided, *but good and bad both, it's time to put them away. It's time to put my heart back together.*

Almost imperceptibly, having made this determination, Elizabeth felt her spirits lift. Jessica had one week left with Robert, and Elizabeth had one week, too—one final week in which to enjoy the city and her job and the company of her friends with a clear, healing heart.

One week, Elizabeth thought, taking Rene's hand and leading him out onto the dance floor, *and then I'll be back in Sweet Valley. Back to my real life—the life I love. Back with my family, and Todd. Home.*

Bantam Books in the Sweet Valley High series
Ask your bookseller for the books you have missed

SIGN UP FOR THE SWEET VALLEY HIGH® FAN CLUB!

Hey, girls! Get all the gossip on Sweet Valley High's® most popular teenagers when you join our fantastic Fan Club! As a member, you'll get all of this really cool stuff:

- Membership Card with your own personal Fan Club ID number
- A Sweet Valley High® Secret Treasure Box
- Sweet Valley High® Stationery
- Official Fan Club Pencil (for secret note writing!)
- Three Bookmarks
- A "Members Only" Door Hanger
- Two Skeins of J. & P. Coats® Embroidery Floss with flower barrette instruction leaflet
- Two editions of *The Oracle* newsletter
- Plus exclusive Sweet Valley High® product offers, special savings, contests, and much more!

- -

Be the first to find out what Jessica & Elizabeth Wakefield are up to by joining the Sweet Valley High® Fan Club for the one-year membership fee of only $6.25 each for U.S. residents, $8.25 for Canadian residents (U.S. currency). Includes shipping & handling.

Send a check or money order (do not send cash) made payable to "Sweet Valley High® Fan Club" along with this form to:

SWEET VALLEY HIGH® FAN CLUB, BOX 3919-B, SCHAUMBURG, IL 60168-3919

NAME_____
                                        (Please print clearly)

ADDRESS_____

CITY_____ STATE_____ ZIP_____
                                                          (Required)

AGE_____ BIRTHDAY_____ /_____ /_____